THE
ANGRY
INTRUDER

Christy of Cutter Gap

THE
ANGRY
INTRUDER

Christy® of Cutter Gap

THE SERIES

Based on the novel Christy *by*

CATHERINE MARSHALL

EVERGREEN
— FARM —
an imprint of
GILEAD PUBLISHING

The Angry Intruder: The Christy® of Cutter Gap series
Adapted by C. Archer
Copyright © 1995 by Marshall-LeSourd, LLC

EVERGREEN
— FARM —

Published by Evergreen Farm, an imprint of Gilead Publishing, LLC,
Wheaton, Illinois, USA.
www.gileadpublishing.com/evergreenfarm

Scripture quotations are taken from *The Holy Bible, King James Version.*

This is a work of fiction. Names, characters, places, and incidents are products of the
author's imagination or are used fictitiously. Any similarity to actual people, organizations,
and/or events is purely coincidental.

ISBN: 978-1-68370-161-3 (printed softcover)
ISBN: 978-1-68370-162-0 (ebook)

Cover design by Larry Taylor
Cover illustrations © Larry Taylor. All rights reserved.
Interior design by Beth Shagene
Ebook production by Book Genesis, Inc.

Printed in the United States of America.

18 19 20 21 22 23 24 / 5 4 3 2 1

The Characters

Christy Rudd Huddleston, a nineteen-year-old girl

Christy's students:
   Rob Allen, fourteen
   Creed Allen, nine
   Little Burl Allen, six
   Bessie Coburn, twelve
   Lizette Holcombe, fifteen
   Wraight Holt, seventeen
   Zacharias Holt, nine
   Vella Holt, five
   Smith O'Teale, fifteen
   Mountie O'Teale, ten
   Mary O'Teale, eight
   Ruby May Morrison, thirteen
   John Spencer, fifteen
   Clara Spencer, twelve
   Zady Spencer, ten
   Lulu Spencer, six
   Lundy Taylor, seventeen

Ben Pentland, the mailman

Prince, black stallion donated to the mission

Goldie, mare belonging to Miss Alice Henderson

Old Theo, crippled mule owned by the mission

Lucy Mae Furnam, Prince's former owner

Charles Furnam, her husband

Ozias Holt, a mountain man
(Father of Christy's students, Wraight, Zacharias, and Vella)

Georgie Holt, Ozias's sister

Alice Henderson, a Quaker mission worker from Ardmore, Pennsylvania

David Grantland, the young minister

Ida Grantland, David's sister

Dr. Neil MacNeill, the physician of the Cove

Fairlight Spencer, a mountain woman

Jeb Spencer, her husband
(Parents of Little Guy and Christy's students, John, Clara, Zady, and Lulu.)

Bob Allen, a mountain man

Granny O'Teale, a superstitious mountain woman
(Great-grandmother of Christy's students, Smith, Mountie, and Mary)

One

"Special delivery from the U-nited States Postal Service for Miss Christy Rudd Huddleston!" Ben Pentland, the mailman, waved from the doorway of the one-room schoolhouse where Christy taught.

Her students—all sixty-seven of them—whispered excitedly. The arrival of the mail was always a big event in this remote section of the Great Smoky Mountains.

"Thank you, Mr. Pentland," Christy called. "Why don't you just leave it by the door?"

"Well, Miz Christy, I don't mean to be ornery—" Mr. Pentland stroked his whiskered chin— "but I reckon that's not such a good idea."

"As you can see, we're in the middle of an arithmetic lesson, Mr. Pentland," Christy explained. She pointed to the blackboard, where fifteen-year-old John Spencer was carefully adding a long column of numbers.

"I'm sorry to interrupt your learnin'," Mr. Pentland said, shifting his mail bag from one shoulder to the other, "but this is what you might call a mighty big special delivery."

The students murmured excitedly. "Go on and get it, why don't you, Teacher?" urged Ruby Mae Morrison, a red-haired thirteen-year-old who was the school's biggest gossip.

"We have more important matters to attend to, Ruby Mae," Christy said in a professional tone.

But the truth was she couldn't help wondering what Mr. Pentland had brought. Could it be a package from her parents, back in North Carolina? In her letters home, she had urged them to help her locate much-needed supplies for the mission school. Christy's mother had promised to talk to the women's group at their church about gathering clothing and shoes for the poor mountain children.

Christy had even written several companies about the mission's desperate need for supplies, requesting donations of mattresses, soap, food, window shades, and cleaning supplies. She'd contacted the Bell Telephone Company, asking them to donate wires and equipment for a telephone, since nobody in the area owned one. And although she knew they probably wouldn't answer, she'd even written the Lyon & Healy Company in the hope of obtaining a piano for the mission. Although weeks had passed, none of the companies had responded.

Perhaps, Christy thought excitedly, *this delivery today is the first answer to my letters!*

"I have to admit I'm curious about the delivery, Mr. Pentland," Christy said, "but it would be wrong to interrupt John in the middle of his arithmetic work." John was a gifted student who was especially strong in mathematics. Even before the school had opened, he'd managed to do all the problems in a worn, old geometry textbook by himself.

"Miz Christy," John said, "I could hold off on my figurin', if'n you want to see about the special delivery."

"No, John," Christy replied, "you go ahead and add that last column. By the way, you've done a great job so far. I'm proud of you." She turned to Mr. Pentland. "I'll deal with the mail during the noon recess, Mr. Pentland."

"Truth to tell," Mr. Pentland said, his deep-set eyes gleaming, "I'm not rightly sure the mail will wait that long."

"Is it a big package?" Christy asked.

Mr. Pentland nodded slowly. "Biggest I ever did deliver."

"Where is it now?"

"Over to the back side of the school."

"I wonder if it's from one of the businesses I wrote," Christy said.

"Looks like a donation for the mission, near as I can figure."

"It's not a mattress, is it?"

"No'm." Mr. Pentland grinned. "Although like as not you could sit on it, if'n it were willin'."

"I don't understand—"

"Come on, Teacher," cried Creed Allen, a freckled nine-year-old. "I'm like to burst wide open if'n I don't see what it is!"

"All right, then. Let's just finish up these problems first. John, let me know when you're done. Meanwhile, have the rest of you come up with an answer to the arithmetic problem I assigned? When we add two and four together, we get . . ."

She pointed to Lundy Taylor, a burly seventeen-year-old who was the class bully. "Lundy, if I add two apples and four apples together, how many apples do I have?"

Lundy shrugged. "Enough for a good-sized pie, I reckon,"

The class broke into laughter.

Mr. Pentland rubbed his mouth, not quite hiding a smile.

"Well, to tell you the truth, Lundy, I'm not much of a cook myself," Christy said, "so I'll have to take your word for it. But what I'm looking for now is a number."

Lundy stared at the floor.

"Lordamercy!" Creed cried. "Even I know this one, Teacher!"

"Wraight?" Christy asked. Wraight Holt, also seventeen, was one of Lundy's best friends. "How about you?"

Wraight shifted uncomfortably in his seat.

"Count it out on your fingers. Two plus four. It won't hurt to try. Nobody will laugh at you if you're wrong. Can you at least give me a guess?"

Wraight just rolled his eyes. He had always been sullen and stubborn, but lately he'd been acting even more difficult than usual. About the only time Christy had ever seen Wraight smile was when he was playing his battered old dulcimer, a stringed musical instrument. He'd brought it to school with him for a while, but she hadn't seen him with it lately.

"Teacher, I'm done with my figurin'," John announced.

"Just a second, John," Christy said. "Wraight? Imagine the four strings on your dulcimer. What if you added two more? How many would you have then?"

"Ain't never had no extra strings on my dulcimer."

"Pretend, then."

Wraight's nine-year-old brother, Zach, leaned over. Holding his dirty red cap in front of his mouth, he whispered something to Wraight.

Wraight glared at Christy. "I reckon there'd be six."

"That's right, Wraight," Christy said with a tolerant smile. "Or perhaps I should say Zach. Don't worry, those of you who are still having trouble with numbers. Soon you'll be adding just as fast as John does."

As she turned back to her desk, Christy sighed. Usually David Grantland, the mission's young minister, handled math and Bible study classes. But he was busy today with church matters, so Christy had agreed to teach all the classes. It was going to be a very long day.

Christy found teaching students in so many different grades very difficult. When she'd volunteered to teach here at the mission in Cutter Gap, Tennessee, she hadn't realized that her classroom would be filled with over five dozen children ranging in age from five to seventeen. She had a few gifted students who had already been exposed to some schooling— students like John Spencer and Lizette Holcombe, a tall, dark-haired girl of fifteen with intelligent brown eyes. But she also had many students like Lundy Taylor and Wraight Holt, who had never set foot in a classroom before. Christy didn't want to bore the more advanced students. On the other hand, she didn't want to discourage the ones who'd never been to school before.

"John, let's go over those figures in a moment," Christy said. She smiled at Mr. Pentland. "I suppose our curiosity is getting the better of us. Why don't you bring the package in here so we can all take a look at it?"

"You're sure about wantin' it in here?"

"If it's a donation for the mission, why not? The children will enjoy seeing what you've brought."

"Oh, I reckon they'll enjoy it, all right." Chuckling softly to himself, Mr. Pentland set down his bag and headed off.

Christy couldn't help feeling proud of herself. After only two months of teaching, she'd managed to obtain much-needed supplies for the mission school—and all on her own. Even Miss Alice Henderson, who'd helped found the school, hadn't thought of writing to companies for donations. Miss Alice was going to be very impressed when she saw the results of Christy's efforts.

It would be nice, Christy thought, *if this first package contained donated books. Won't it be wonderful for each child to have a fresh, new book to hold—*

She gasped.

Mr. Pentland stood in the doorway, grinning from ear to ear. "Like I said, biggest delivery I ever did make. Hungriest too. Ate half my lunch on the way here."

Slowly Mr. Pentland entered the room. He was pulling on a rope. Attached to the rope was a huge black stallion with a white star on his forehead. The horse had a silky mane and a long, flowing tail. On his back sat a beautiful leather saddle.

The horse had to lower his proud head to come in through the door. His hooves pounded on the wooden floor. When he tossed his tail, it whipped back and forth across the faces of the students on the last row. Gazing curiously at the class, he snorted twice. His ears twitched. Then he leaned down to nuzzle Ruby Mae's hair.

"Her hair's so red, he most likely figures it's carrots," Mr. Pentland joked.

"Mr. Pentland," Christy said when she finally managed to recover her voice, "there must be some mistake. This is . . . this is a horse!"

Mr. Pentland grinned. "For a city gal, you sure do pick

things up quick-like. Bet you can even tell which end of the horse is which."

"Well, I am a city gal," Christy said with a laugh, "but I'm pretty sure you feed the end without a tail." She shook her head. "But I still say there's got to be some mistake. When I requested donations, I didn't ask for a horse. Did he come with a note, or any kind of explanation?"

"Just that tag on his saddle with your name on it."

"But Teacher," said Zach, "the mission needs a horse bad. All you got is that half-crippled mule, Old Theo."

It was true. Miss Alice owned a horse, but she was often gone on long trips. Without any transportation, it was very difficult for David to visit families living in remote areas.

"You're right, Zach," Christy agreed. "But we still can't keep this horse."

The entire class moaned in disappointment. As if he understood what was going on, the horse stepped closer to Christy's desk, his hooves clopping loudly on the floor. He nudged Christy's shoulder.

"I reckon he likes you, Teacher," said Mary O'Teale, a gentle eight-year-old with wide green eyes. The horse's tail swished over her face as he tossed it to and fro.

"I'm sure you're a very nice horse," Christy said to the stallion, "but we can't keep you without knowing where you came from."

"I plumb forgot," Mr. Pentland exclaimed. "You've got a couple letters too. Had a monstrous big pile of mail this week. Eight whole letters." He stroked the horse's neck. "Nine, if'n you count this big, hairy one."

Christy smiled. She still couldn't get over living in a world where eight letters meant a "big pile of mail."

Mr. Pentland handed Christy the letters. One was from her mother. The other had a North Carolina postmark, too, but Christy didn't recognize the name on the envelope.

She opened it and read:

February 8, 1912

Dear Miss Huddleston:

I hope that you will forgive a stranger writing to you. Let me explain that I have just returned from Asheville, where I was visiting my sister.

At a tea she gave in my honor, I met your mother. She spoke most charmingly about the contents of some of your recent letters, your fascinating pupils, and their needs.

When she mentioned the mission's need for a good horse, my heart soared, for I knew of the perfect animal. My husband, Charles, having developed rheumatism this past year, has been unable to give our fine stallion, Prince, the exercise and attention he properly deserves. I trust that the mission will find him the loving friend and companion that we have.

> *Sincerely,*
> *Lucy Mae*
> *Furnam*

Christy stroked the horse's glossy mane. "Well, Prince," she said, "it looks like you have a new home."

"You're a-keepin' him for sure and certain?" Ruby Mae cried.

"It seems he is a gift," Christy explained, "from some people back in my home state. His name is Prince."

"And he looks like one, don't he, Teacher?" asked Little Burl Allen, a sweet, red-haired six-year-old.

"Yes, he does, Little Burl," Christy agreed. "Very majestic. All he needs is a crown."

"Can Ruby Mae and me ride him double-like?" asked Bessie Coburn. Twelve-year-old Bessie was Ruby Mae's best friend.

"I think what Prince needs right now is a little rest after his long journey," Christy said.

But just then Prince reared up on his hind legs.

"Look out!" Ruby Mae yelled.

The horse's black head nearly touched the rafters as he pawed the air with his forelegs.

"Whoa, there, boy," Mr. Pentland soothed, pulling on the lead rope. At last Prince lowered his legs. He stood calmly, as if nothing unusual had happened.

"No, ma'am," Little Burl said, shaking his head. "I don't reckon he is tired."

Christy laughed, a little flustered by the sudden display. "Well, we'd better take Prince outside."

Ruby Mae and Bessie jumped up to grab the lead rope. Prince, with his head still high, allowed himself to be led through the door. Christy, Mr. Pentland, and the rest of the children followed behind.

As soon as he was out on the snow-covered grass, the horse yanked free of the girls' grasp and took off at a gallop. He ran in a great, wide circle, tossing his head back and forth and kicking up sprays of snow. Finally, after several minutes, he meekly returned to the children.

"Thank you, Mr. Pentland, for bringing him all this way," Christy said. "He really is a beauty."

"All part of bein' a U-nited States mailman," Mr. Pentland said with a tip of his worn hat. "Anyways, kind of liked having a critter around for company. By the way, I 'spect there's more surprises a-comin'. Big delivery come into El Pano yesterday. Should be here soon."

Ruby Mae tugged on Mr. Pentland's sleeve. "Another horse?"

"Nope," he said with a sly grin.

"We'll let it be a surprise," Christy said. "Just tell me this, so I can prepare myself: does it breathe?"

"Nope. Don't breathe," said Mr. Pentland. "'Course it do make noise . . ." With a mysterious smile, he was on his way.

As Christy watched him leave, she realized she felt a real fondness for the gentle mailman. Mr. Pentland had escorted Christy on her seven-mile journey through the mountains when she came to Cutter Gap two months ago. It had been a rough trip, ending with Christy's fall into a dangerous, icy river. Through it all, Mr. Pentland had been a kind friend when she'd needed one.

"Ruby Mae," Christy said, "why don't you and Bessie take Prince over to the mission house? I believe I saw Mr. Grantland over there. He'll take care of our new friend."

Christy turned back toward the school. A snowball fight had already started. If she didn't get everyone back into the classroom soon, she'd lose what little control she had.

"All right, now," Christy called loudly. "Back to John's math problems."

The children responded with loud groans. A few of her more willing students, like John and Lizette, rushed up the steps to the schoolhouse.

Wouldn't it be wonderful, Christy thought, *if all my students were so eager and quick to learn?*

Unfortunately, most of them had never even handled a

pencil or a piece of chalk or a real book. And without the necessary supplies, there were days when Christy wondered if she would ever make a difference in the lives of her young students.

Still, Prince's unexpected arrival had filled her with hope. She couldn't exactly take credit for the beautiful horse; he was a surprise gift, after all. But if some of the other donations she'd requested came through—to think of all the changes she could make to the mission school! She couldn't wait to see what the next delivery would bring.

"Miz Christy! Come quick!" Lizette called from the doorway.

"What is it, Lizette?"

"Somebody's done erased all of John's figurin'. And there's ink spilled all over your papers!"

Rounding up the last few stragglers, Christy hurried inside the school. A deep-blue puddle of ink covered her attendance book. It flowed to the edge of her desk, where it dripped like a tiny waterfall onto the rough, wood floor. John stood by the blackboard, staring in dismay at the smeared remains of his addition problems. The ghosts of a few numbers were still visible, but most of his work had been completely erased.

Christy wondered if Prince had somehow knocked over her inkwell. But no, the horse hadn't been near her desk when he'd reared up. And he certainly hadn't erased the board.

"Sit down, all of you," Christy called. Reining in her anger, she lowered her voice. "Please go to your seats. I need to get to the bottom of this."

She heard snickers outside. She leaned out the door to see a group of the older boys—Lundy Taylor, Smith O'Teale,

Wraight Holt, and Wraight's little brother Zach—hovering near the steps, whispering.

"Inside, now!" Christy ordered.

The boys sauntered in, taking their time. Zach, a thin boy with curly blond hair, cast a nervous glance in Christy's direction, then slipped into his seat. Lundy chuckled as he walked to his desk.

"I'm glad you find this so amusing, Lundy," Christy said. "But I'm afraid I do not. John worked very hard on those math problems. And as for my attendance book, it's ruined. Do you realize how difficult it is for us to obtain supplies? Ink and paper and chalk cost money."

Christy paced up and down the aisles of the small classroom. An uneasy quiet fell over the class. Some students hung their heads. Others looked out the windows. Lundy, Wraight, and Smith avoided her gaze.

"I want to know who did this," Christy said. "And I want to know right now."

She was not surprised when no one answered.

After a tense moment, John raised his hand. "Miz Christy, I can do the figurin' again. It ain't no problem."

"That's not the point, John. I need to find out who is responsible for this."

Actually, Christy had a pretty good idea who the culprit was: Lundy Taylor. Although she'd never been able to prove it, she was certain that Lundy had thrown a rock at five-year-old Vella Holt on the first day of school. It was also likely that he'd tripped Mary O'Teale at the top of an icy slide, causing her to tumble down a steep slope and hurt her arm and head. But no one would ever directly accuse Lundy of anything. He was big and hulking and mean, and even Christy was a little afraid of him.

"Lundy, do you have anything to say?" Christy asked.

"I'd say you got yourself one big mess up yonder on that desk," Lundy said with a smirk.

Christy clenched her hands. She took a deep breath. She was determined not to lose her temper.

"It's just some spilled ink," she said. "I'll clean it up. John will redo his arithmetic. And that's that. But if I ever catch one of you vandalizing the school again, I'll—" She lowered her voice. "This is your school. It belongs to you. You should treat it with respect and love."

Christy put a fresh column of numbers on the blackboard for John. But as she wrote, she couldn't help glancing back at Lundy. He glared back with steely dark eyes. What else was Lundy capable of doing to the school?

It's just a prank, nothing more, Christy told herself, but she couldn't quite bring herself to believe it.

Two

When school was over, Lizette offered to stay behind and help clean up the classroom.

"I'd be glad for the help," said Christy, "and the company." Lizette couldn't help beaming.

She loved the way Miz Christy talked, so nice and citified. And Miz Christy had a sweetness to her that Lizette admired. She often tried to picture herself as a teacher someday, just like Miz Christy, with fine clothes and pleasant manners and so much learning inside her head.

Lizette took the blackboard erasers outside to bang them together. The chalk dust exploded in big puffs and floated away on the breeze.

Just then, she spotted a scene that sent her heart leaping straight into her throat. Lundy, Smith, and Wraight were standing shoulder to shoulder by the edge of the woods. Wraight's little brother, Zach, stood a few steps back, looking worried.

John Spencer stood alone, facing the three older boys.

Lizette strained to listen. She could hear angry voices—especially Lundy's.

"I'll knock you good, if'n you don't keep your trap shut," Lundy was saying.

John said something in response, but Lizette couldn't tell what it was. She wondered if she should go back inside and get Miz Christy. It looked like things could turn ugly, right quick. No doubt Miz Christy could put an end to it all with a few words.

But Teacher wouldn't always be around every time Lundy Taylor decided to act like a bully.

Lizette made up her mind. Trying to look as tough as Miz Christy did when she had words with Lundy, she strode over to the boys. Lundy saw her coming and gave a nasty laugh. "Look'a here, John. Lizette is a-comin' to rescue you."

John did not turn around. He just scowled and stood his ground. But Lizette could tell he was plenty scared. She tried to meet Wraight's gaze. But Wraight was looking straight ahead, his eyes dark with anger.

Why does Wraight get so angry sometimes? Lizette wondered. Wraight wasn't like Lundy. Not really, not deep down.

"John, Teacher was wonderin' if'n you was still here, and if maybe you could go back and help her with somethin'," Lizette lied in a shaky voice.

"Maybe you'd best run along and hide behind Teacher's skirts, John," Lundy sneered.

"I'm just warning you, Lundy," John said. "You shouldn't go messin' up Teacher's things."

Lundy stepped closer, until his chest was right up against John's. "You're warnin' me? I'll do what I please with Teacher. If'n I want, I might just get rid of her, permanent-like. That city gal's got no business here in the Cove. You hear me, boy?" He balled up his fist, ready to strike. "I believe it's time you was taught a real lesson."

"Lundy, don't!" Lizette cried.

"'Lundy, don't! Lundy, don't!'" Lundy mocked her.

Suddenly, the glint of anger in Wraight's eyes flickered. He glanced at Lizette. "Let him go, Lundy," he said in a low voice. Lizette sent him a grateful look.

"Let him go?" Lundy demanded. "Well, Wraight, it was you who was made a fool of by this little teacher's pet, a-showin' off in class. Him and all his figurin'."

Now the black anger raged in Wraight's eyes. He seemed to be fighting with it. "It weren't John's fault," he said at last. He jerked his head back toward the schoolhouse. "It's that flatlander teacher who's got everything all mixed up."

Lundy looked annoyed. He shoved John away with both hands. "I reckon you get to live another day, teacher's pet. Run on to Miz Christy, now. That's where you belong."

Lizette could tell how angry John was. But it was clear he saw no point in starting a fight he was sure to lose. Slowly, he turned away.

"You'd best go, too, Lizette," Lundy said with a sneer. "Two of a kind, you and John. Two little teacher's pets." With a last snort, Lundy turned away, followed by Smith.

Wraight began to follow them, but Lizette grabbed his arm. He looked at her, surprised. Silently, so that only Wraight would know what she said, she mouthed the words, "Thank you."

For a second, the anger in Wraight's eyes was truly gone. In its place was something gentler, a look Lizette had seen before.

"Lizette?" Miz Christy called.

Wraight looked past Lizette to the schoolhouse. Once more, the dark shadow settled over his face. He turned and followed Lundy and Smith into the woods, followed at a distance by his little brother.

⌐#⌐

Late that night, Christy awoke to the sound of pounding. She sat up in bed, rubbing her eyes. *Tap. Tap. Tap.* No doubt about it. It was the steady, sharp sound of a hammer hitting a nail.

She ran to her window and pulled back the curtain. The wooden floor was icy. The light of a full moon spilled over the snow-covered mission yard.

Who could be hammering in the middle of the night? Was David doing some kind of emergency repair on the school?

Just beyond the school, Christy noticed a small figure dashing into the thick trees. It looked like a little boy. Christy couldn't tell who it was, but she did catch a glimpse of the red cap the boy was wearing.

Zach Holt? What could he be doing here, in the middle of the night? Perhaps someone in the Holt family was sick or hurt. Christy had heard that Ozias Holt, Zach's father, sometimes drank too much. Maybe it wasn't hammering she'd heard. Maybe Zach had been pounding at the front door, trying to get Christy to wake up. But why had he given up and run away so quickly?

Christy put on her robe and slippers. She met Miss Ida, David's older, no-nonsense sister, at the top of the stairs. Miss Ida was carrying a lamp and wearing a nightgown, with a knitted shawl draped over her shoulders. It seemed strange to see her gray hair hanging loose. Usually she wore it in a tight bun.

"What on earth was that banging?" Miss Ida asked, rubbing her eyes.

"I thought I saw one of my students by the schoolhouse," Christy said. "Let's go take a look."

Miss Ida led the way down the stairs. The lamp cast long, dancing shadows on the walls. Walking side by side, Christy and Miss Ida crossed the main room.

The mission house was a white three-story frame building with a screened porch on either side. Miss Ida and Christy lived there along with Ruby Mae, who had been having problems at home and needed a temporary place to stay. Miss Alice had her own cabin, and David had a bunkhouse nearby. The house was primitive, with no electricity, telephone, or indoor plumbing, and only the barest of furnishings. Still, Christy had already begun to think of it as her real home.

"I thought maybe someone was knocking on the door," Christy said. "Maybe Zach needed help, and when no one answered, he ran off."

"No," Miss Ida said firmly. "That was hammering I heard, I'm certain of it."

"Maybe David was doing some repairs on the schoolhouse."

"In the middle of the night? Nonsense."

Christy opened the front door. Cold air slapped at her like an icy hand. It was March, but the mountain nights were nearly as bitter as they had been in January when Christy had first arrived at the mission.

She stepped out onto the porch. The yard was covered with muddy patches of snow. Up the hill stood the newly built schoolhouse, which also served as a church on Sundays. In the silvery moonlight, the freshly painted building practically glowed. A gust of wind set the tree branches chattering.

"I don't see anything," Miss Ida said.

"Or anyone," Christy added in a whisper. She turned to Miss Ida. "You wait here. It's awfully cold. I'll go take a look."

"Take my shawl," Miss Ida said. "And be careful."

Slowly, Christy crossed the yard. The snow patches were crusty and packed. *I wish I'd worn my boots*, she thought. Instantly she felt guilty. The little footprints of her students filled the yard. Few of the children owned shoes. Even in the coldest weather, they walked to school barefoot.

The sight of an especially small set of footprints, glowing in the moonlight, filled Christy with a mixture of love and awe. The school meant so much to these children that they would walk for miles through snow-covered mountains just to spend a few hours here. It showed just how much they wanted to learn—

Christy froze in place as the front of the school came clearly into view. "No!" she cried in outrage.

The message was scrawled across the front of the school in huge, dripping brown letters:

GIT AWA TEECHR

Hugging Miss Ida's shawl to herself, Christy stared in disbelief at the crude writing. "'Get away, Teacher,'" she whispered, nearly choking on the words.

She stepped closer, touching her index finger to one of the letters. It wasn't paint. But it was an oily, smelly goop that certainly wouldn't wash off easily.

She heard steps behind her and spun around, her heart racing.

"Christy?" came a familiar voice. "What is it?"

Miss Alice walked across the yard. She was wearing a blue coat over her nightgown. Her long, thick hair, sprinkled with gray, hung down past her shoulders. Even now, awakened from sleep in the middle of the night, she walked like a magnificent queen, tall and dignified.

Miss Alice shook her head sadly as she draped her arm around Christy's shoulders. "It's terrible," she murmured as she gazed at the words scrawled across the wood. "Just terrible."

"Isn't it?" Christy cried. "How could someone do such a thing?"

Miss Alice gave a wry smile. "No, I meant the spelling."

"How can you make jokes?" Christy moaned.

"I find that laughter is almost always the best way to deal with a difficult problem," Miss Alice said. She climbed the steps to the front door and pointed. "This explains the hammering."

For the first time, Christy noticed the long piece of wood nailed across the doorframe. "But why would anyone do that?" she cried.

"To keep us out, I imagine," Miss Alice said calmly. "It's a simple enough thing to remove the nails, of course. Not a very well-planned prank."

"Is that all you think it is?" Christy asked. "A prank?"

Miss Alice examined the nailed board. "Most likely."

"Are you two all right?" a male voice called from the distance.

Christy craned her neck. It was David, dashing across the

yard. He was wearing big boots and long johns. His black hair was a tangled mess. She couldn't help grinning. He looked a little ridiculous.

"David to the rescue," she teased.

David rushed up the stairs, panting. He combed a hand through his snarled hair, but one stubborn lock still poked into the air. "It's a long way from the bunkhouse, you know," he said sheepishly. "I came as fast as I could."

"Nice outfit," Christy said. "A little flashy for Cutter Gap."

David started to respond, but just then he noticed the words scrawled over the schoolhouse. "What—" He rubbed his eyes. His mouth hung open.

"Miss Alice thinks it's a prank," Christy said.

David ran a finger over one of the letters. "What is this stuff?"

"A mixture of things, probably," Miss Alice said. "Goodness knows no one around here can afford paint. I'd guess some lard, some mud, maybe some of the homemade dye the women use for coloring yarn. Could be any number of things."

"My beautiful paint job," David moaned.

"They nailed the door shut too," Christy said.

David rolled his eyes. "Well, that's easy enough to remedy, at least."

"Let's get inside before we all end up with frostbite," Miss Alice said. "We can take care of this mess before school starts in the morning."

Christy shook her head. "I don't want to clean it off."

"But we have to," David insisted.

"No. I want the children to see what someone has done to their school."

"Come to think of it, that's probably a good idea, Christy," David agreed. "Maybe someone will even confess. I doubt it, though."

"Let's get over to the house and warm up with some tea," Miss Alice urged.

"First I want to check on Prince," David said. "It's his first night here, and I want to make sure he's doing all right."

"I'll go too," Christy said.

Miss Alice grinned. "Might as well make a night of it."

The little shed that served as a barn was dark and cozy. It smelled of leather and hay, a soothing, warm scent. Christy went over to Prince, who eyed her sleepily. She stroked his velvety muzzle.

"How do you like your new home, Prince?" she asked.

"Seems to like it fine," David said. "He and Goldie are already good friends. Old Theo, I'm not so sure about."

"Isn't he beautiful, Miss Alice?" Christy asked.

"He is indeed," Miss Alice said.

Christy rubbed her cheek against the stallion's warm neck. What an unexpected gift he was! His arrival had made Christy all the more anxious to receive responses to her letters. Miss Alice was going to be so surprised. She didn't know about the letters Christy had sent requesting donations from businesses.

It wasn't that Christy wanted to keep them from Miss Alice. But there was no point in discussing her plan, she told herself, until she saw the results. Then it would be a real surprise.

Christy's thoughts turned back to tonight's disturbing incident.

"Well, it looks as if everything's in order here," David said. "Let's go have that tea."

"It'll be dawn soon," Miss Alice said. "Perhaps we should just have breakfast."

"Coming, Christy?" David asked from the doorway of the shed.

Christy stroked Prince's ear distractedly.

"Oh—yes. Sorry. I was just thinking about the writing on the school. Why would someone write that about me? It's hard not to take it personally. I keep thinking about Zach, wondering if I've hurt him in some way . . ."

"Zach Holt?" David repeated. "Why him?"

"I thought I saw him running from the school," Christy explained. "Or at least I saw his red cap. But the more I think about it, the more I can't believe it was Zach. For one thing, some of those letters are very high. A fairly tall person had to write them."

David nodded. "Good point. Unless, of course, Zach was sitting on the shoulders of a friend."

"Or using stilts," Miss Alice added with a grin.

"There's another reason I doubt it was Zach," Christy said.

"And what is that, Sherlock Holmes?" David inquired, arms crossed over his chest.

"Elementary, my dear Watson. Zach Holt just happens to be a very fine speller. He would never spell 'teacher' with two *e*'s."

Miss Alice laughed. "With you on the case, we're sure to get to the bottom of this prank."

"I hope that's all it is," David said, his voice tensing.

"What do you mean, David?"

"Well, Zach's been spending a lot of time with the older

troublemakers—his brother, Wraight, as well as Lundy and Smith. They're capable of making more than simple mischief." He stared at Christy thoughtfully. "I just think you should be careful for the next few days."

Christy smiled. It was sweet, and a little flattering, that David was acting so protective. Still, she could take care of herself. "I'll be fine, David. I'm a big girl."

"After all those problems with Granny O'Teale, though," David said, "there may still be some bad feelings about you."

Christy shuddered at the memory. She had only been teaching for a week when Granny O'Teale, the great-grandmother of the six O'Teale children, had started a terrible rumor about Christy. She'd decided that Christy was cursed after a big black raven flew into the schoolroom and perched next to Christy on her desk.

"Let's not jump to any conclusions, David," Miss Alice advised. "Maybe this is just a one-time incident. Has anything else happened at school like this?"

"No . . ." Christy began. She hesitated. "Well, come to think of it, today someone erased some of John Spencer's arithmetic problems off the board and spilled ink on my attendance book."

"You be careful, Christy," David said. "These aren't all just innocent children. The mountain people have been raised to think that feuding and fighting are part of daily life."

"There is good in all these people, David," Miss Alice chided gently. "And in all God's creatures. Sometimes we just have to look a little harder."

David nodded. "I know that, Miss Alice. But that doesn't mean Christy shouldn't watch herself. Things could get out of hand, even if this prankster doesn't mean for them to."

"Stop worrying, David," Christy said with a wave of her hand. "I'll take care of myself, I promise. Besides, I have more important things to worry about."

"Such as?" David asked.

"Such as how I'm ever going to teach these children how to spell correctly!"

"See how things go today," Miss Alice said. "We'll talk more after school at dinner."

"Oh, that reminds me," Christy said. "I promised Fairlight Spencer I'd start teaching her reading this afternoon. I may be a little late getting home." Fairlight Spencer was the mother of four of Christy's students—John, Clara, Zady, and Lulu.

"Well, just be careful coming home from the Spencers' cabin," David advised. "That's a long walk, and it gets dark early, you know. Maybe I should walk you home."

"I'll have John walk me home," Christy promised.

"All right, then," David agreed.

The three of them left the shed and made their way across the yard. Christy glanced back over her shoulder at the school. "'Get away, Teacher,'" she murmured.

Prank or not, the words still stung.

Three

By the time the children arrived for school that morning, David had removed the plank nailed across the schoolhouse door. As the students read the message scrawled on the front of the school, Christy watched their expressions, hoping to get a clue about the culprit. She kept a careful eye on Lundy, Smith, and Wraight. Lundy seemed to find the message especially funny, but that was hardly proof he was involved.

When Zach arrived, trailing behind the older boys, he just glanced at the message for a moment, then turned away. He pulled his dirty red cap down so low that his eyes were almost hidden.

"It's the most all-fired rotten thing I ever did see, Miz Christy," cried Lizette. Her wide brown eyes glistened with tears. "Makes me madder'n a peeled rattler to see something like that on our brand-spankin' new school. Who do you think done it?"

Christy patted Lizette's shoulder. "I'm not sure, Lizette," she said. "But I intend to find out."

"Let's clean it off," John suggested.

"We will," Christy said, "but first I want everybody to have a look."

A tiny, cold hand reached for Christy's. It was Mountie O'Teale, a shy ten-year-old who, with Christy's help, was learning to overcome a speech problem that had left her nearly silent.

"But Teacher," Mountie said softly. "I—it was so purty and clean."

Christy smiled. Every time Mountie spoke, it still seemed like a small miracle. "I know, Mountie," she said. "But we'll fix the school. Don't worry, sweetheart. Soon it'll be good as new."

When all the students had arrived, Christy signaled for them to quiet down and gather by the school. "First things first," she said to her hushed audience. She knelt down and dipped her hand into a slushy spot of half-frozen mud near the steps, scooping up a big handful.

"What in tarnation are you doin', Miz Christy?" Ruby Mae cried.

"Mud fight!" Creed yelled, and some of the other boys cheered.

"Nice try, Creed," Christy said. "But this mud is for another purpose."

Lifting her long skirt, Christy picked her way along the edge of the building through the snow and mud.

"She's gone plumb crazy, I 'spect," Ruby Mae whispered loudly.

Christy turned to the group. *"Laughter is almost always the best way to deal with a difficult problem,"* Miss Alice had said.

"I want to say that while I appreciate the effort that went into this . . . this little writing exercise, I am very disappointed in the spelling." Christy turned to the wall. "To begin with, it's 'g-e-t,' not 'g-i-t.'"

Using the cold mud, Christy carefully drew three small horizontal lines extending from the letter *i*. Behind her, the children watched, murmuring and whispering in amazement. A few giggled.

"And the rest of this is no better." Christy corrected the remaining message as well as she could. She glanced back at her students. Most of them were staring at her mud-covered hand.

"And frankly, I don't much care for the punctuation," Christy added. "I would add a comma here, after 'away.' And how about an exclamation point at the end? That way—" she paused to smile— "it's clear you're serious about wanting me to leave."

Christy stepped back to admire her work:

GET AWAY, TEACHER!

"There," she said with satisfaction. "Much better. I want to thank the person responsible for providing us with such an excellent opportunity for a spelling lesson. Next time, however, if it's not too much trouble, I'd prefer to work on grammar." Christy motioned to the door. "Time to head inside."

"But Teacher," came a small voice.

Christy felt a tug at her skirt. It was Little Burl.

"What is it, Little Burl?"

"Ain't you mad? About the writin'?"

Christy smiled. "Sometimes getting mad just gets in the way, Little Burl. I'm disappointed that somebody hurt the new school. And I'm sad to think that someone is angry at me because I would never want to hurt one of you in any way. Not ever."

"But what about the mess?" Creed asked. "Who's a-goin' to clean it off?"

Christy winked. "Guess what we're going to be doing during noon recess?"

Everyone groaned.

"If I ever get my hands on the person who did this, I'll whop him good!" Creed said.

"I appreciate the offer, Creed," Christy said. "But I don't think that'll be necessary. The person who did this knows that it was wrong. And I hope that he—or she—will reconsider before pulling a similar stunt. Now I want all of you to get inside. I'll be there in a minute. I've got to wash off my hand in the snow."

While the children made their way up the steps, Christy knelt and wiped her muddy hand in a patch of snow. When Zach passed, she motioned for him to join her. He grimaced, glanced over at his brother, then reluctantly shuffled over. Wraight, Lundy, and Smith waited for him by the door, scowling at Christy.

"Zach," Christy said in a soft voice so the others wouldn't hear, "you know that I would never accuse you of something unless I had a very good reason, don't you?"

Zach shrugged. He kicked at a mound of snow with his bare foot.

"The thing is I thought I saw someone running away from the school last night. He was about your size, and he had on a red cap, just like the one you're wearing."

Zach touched his cap. His cheeks were flushed. "Don't mean nothin'," he finally said. "Sure don't mean I done it."

Christy stood and dried her hand on her skirt. "No, it doesn't. As a matter of fact, I happen to know from your work that you're an excellent speller, Zach. You would never spell 'Teacher' the way it was written on the wall."

A small smile lit up Zach's thin face. "Got to admit it ain't the best spellin' I ever seen, that's for certain."

"How did you learn to spell so well, Zach?"

"My Aunt Georgia came a-visitin' last summer. She had a real live book with her. Taught me some of the words. Little ones, leastways."

"That's wonderful. You should be very proud."

Zach shifted from one foot to the other. He glanced nervously toward the door of the schoolhouse. "I reckon so. But just 'cause a feller can't spell and such, that don't mean he's worthless or nothin'."

Christy nodded thoughtfully. Was Zach trying to tell her something? "Zach, I don't think you wrote that, but I do think you might know who did. Can you tell me who it was?"

"Don't know nothin' about that."

"Are you sure?"

Again Zach stole a fearful glance toward the steps, where the older boys were waiting. "Yep."

"Is someone making you afraid, Zach? One of the older boys?"

"I ain't afraid of nobody!" Zach cried. "Now can I go in?"

Christy sighed. "Of course you can." She watched the boy march into the school. "Lundy," she called.

Lundy glared at her. "You be wantin' somethin'?"

"I want to know if you have anything to say about the writing on the school wall."

"I ain't got nothin' to say to you," he spat. Wraight and Smith came to stand beside him.

By now Christy was used to Lundy's angry outbursts. From the first day of school, he'd been this way. But the sneer on his face today was almost more than she could bear. Still, she reminded herself, she wasn't going to get anywhere by yelling at Lundy—even if she did suspect he was responsible for the vandalism.

"I'm just going to ask once. Do you boys know anything about that writing?" Christy questioned calmly.

"Why are you blamin' us?" Wraight demanded. He was a taller version of Zach, with the same gray-blue eyes and tangled blond hair. But there was something troubling in his gaze.

"I'm not blaming you. I just—"

"Why don't you ask Rob Allen or John Spencer if'n they done it?" Wraight pressed, his anger growing.

"'Cause they can spell," Smith said with a snort. "Myself, I don't take no stock in spellin' and such. Can't feed an empty stomach with no spellin' words."

"Boys," Christy said. "I thought you might know something—"

"You know we don't know nothin'," Wraight shot back. His words burned with angry sarcasm. "Nothin'. Can't add, can't spell. Can't do nothin', ain't worth nothin'."

"'Course," Lundy said with a dark smile, "we can shoot the eye out of a deer half a mile aways, quicker than you can spit and holler howdy."

"True enough," Smith agreed.

"What do you think of that, Teacher?" Lundy demanded.

"I think," Christy said with all the quiet force she could muster, "that it's time for you boys to go inside."

As they slowly entered the school, big and sullen and full of anger, Christy suddenly felt very small and afraid. She shivered, but she knew it wasn't because of the cold.

⌒

Lizette just couldn't understand it. If she were the teacher, she would have been angry with the person who'd ruined the front of the school that way. But Miz Christy was sitting at her desk like always, acting as if nothing out of the ordinary had happened. She was reading from a book about a boy named Huckleberry Finn. It was a mighty funny book, and Lizette loved listening to the pretty words. Miz Christy spun them out like pure music.

But Lizette had other things on her mind today. She glanced down at her little blackboard. She'd carefully drawn a heart, with fancy frills along the outside. It was a little lop-sided, but still, it wasn't a bad-looking heart, not at all.

John Spencer had carved a heart just like it on the big spruce near the bridge over Big Spoon Creek. He'd worked on it for two afternoons to get it just so. At least, that's what he'd told Lizette. Inside the heart he'd put big letters: *J. S. + L. H.* It had taken her a minute to realize that the *L. H.* stood for her—Lizette Holcombe.

John had been so proud of his work that Lizette hadn't known what to say. She hated to hurt anyone's feelings, least of all John's. He was probably the nicest boy this side of the Mississippi. But it had taken her by surprise to learn he was sweet on her.

After all, she and John had known each other all their lives. They'd always been friends. Just friends. Always liked the same sorts of things too—dreaming about the future or staring up at the night sky when the stars were just starting to peek out.

Both of them loved learning too. Since school had started, they'd spent long hours talking about how exciting it all was and wondering about the arithmetic and history and English Miz Christy was going to teach them.

And it wasn't that John wasn't a fine-looking boy. He had that curly blond hair, and light brown eyes that smiled a lot. Still, he wasn't the one she couldn't seem to stop thinking about.

Lizette fingered her chalk, considering. In the center of the heart, she wrote *L. H. + W. H.*

Ruby Mae leaned over. "What's that you're writin'?" she whispered.

"Nothin," Lizette said quickly. She wiped away the initials with her palm.

When John had showed her the heart in the spruce tree, his face had turned as red as an apple. "I guess you can tell I'm sweet on you, Lizette," he'd said, all shy and soft.

What could she say? After a while, she'd answered, "I like you, too, I reckon, John," because they'd seemed like words that wouldn't hurt his feelings. But on the way home, when he'd tried to hold her hand, she'd stuffed it in her skirt pocket as fast as lightning. He hadn't tried again after that.

She couldn't have said the real truth of it: that she had her eyes on another boy. To begin with, John probably wouldn't have believed her. Wraight Holt was as different from Lizette as night was from day—on the outside, anyway. Where she liked to talk, he was gruff and shy. Where she loved to learn, he didn't much seem to like school at all. And though it pained her to say it, he wasn't very quick at picking up things, not the way she and John were.

Of course, she'd spent a little bit of time last year at the school way over in Low Gap. The school year only lasted four months there, but that was something, anyway. Wraight hadn't gone to the Low Gap school. His pa wasn't much for learning, from what Lizette could figure. He'd only let the Holt children go to school this year because Wraight's ma had talked him into it.

But Lizette knew that Wraight was smart. Maybe he wasn't the quickest study when it came to letters and numbers and such. Many times she'd seen how angry he got when he looked foolish in class. But Wraight was special in other ways.

He'd long been famous around these parts for his hunting. He'd shot a deer at two hundred yards. And once he'd even brought down a bear that was charging straight at him. Other children had looked up to him after that. Even the men would nod their heads and say, "That Wraight's a tough one, he is, and a mighty fine shot."

But that wasn't all. When Wraight played his dulcimer and sang in a voice so pure it could melt a frozen river, that's when Lizette knew for sure how different he was from all the other boys. And when he smiled at her in a way that made her toes curl up just so, she was even more certain.

Lizette looked up and was surprised to see Miz Christy had finished her reading. When she got to thinking about Wraight like that, Lizette often lost track of time.

Miz Christy was so beautiful. Lizette would give anything to have eyes that blue and a smile that bright. She had a feeling the preacher thought Miz Christy was special too. When he came in the afternoon to teach math and Bible studies, he always had an extra-wide grin for Miz Christy. Anybody with a lick of romance in them could see it there, plain as day.

Ruby Mae had told Lizette she thought Dr. MacNeill was sweet on Miz Christy too. Of course Ruby Mae was full of crazy gossip half the time, but she might just be right about the doctor. She'd sounded pretty sure of herself.

"I have a special announcement to make," Miz Christy said. "I am going to appoint three Junior Teachers today. This is a very special honor. Junior Teachers will help me work with the other students." She held up a small piece of cloth in the shape of a shield. It was trimmed with fancy gold braids and beads. "This is a special badge I made. Each of the Junior Teachers will wear one."

Lizette sat up a little straighter and crossed her fingers. She had never seen anything as beautiful as that badge. Oh, how she wanted to be a Junior Teacher! It was all she could do to keep from waving her hand in the air and begging Miz Christy for the honor.

"John Spencer," Miz Christy announced. John looked over at Lizette and smiled.

"Rob Allen."

Lizette closed her eyes. "Please, please, let it be me," she whispered.

"And Lizette Holcombe," Miz Christy finished. "Come on up and accept your badges."

Lizette gasped. Had Miz Christy really called her name?

"Go on up," Ruby Mae said to Lizette.

Her cheeks flushed, Lizette joined John and Rob at the front of the room. Miz Christy pinned a badge on each of them. John winked at Lizette and nudged her with his elbow. She smiled back, but most of her attention was on her new badge. Miz Christy had made them herself, she'd said. The beads and spangles were as pretty as real diamonds and worth much more to Lizette.

As the Junior Teachers returned to their seats, the class applauded. Lizette glanced toward the back of the room, where she knew Wraight was sitting. Her heart jumped when she realized he was looking right at her. But he didn't return her smile, and he and Lundy and the other boys at the back were not applauding.

Lizette sat down with a sigh. Maybe she was crazy to think Wraight could ever like her. All he'd ever done was throw snowballs at her or tease her a little now and then. But there was that one time he'd sung to her at recess. It had been a song about love and broken hearts and sweet pain, and she'd been almost sure he'd felt something then.

But that had been a while back. Wraight hadn't brought his dulcimer to school in quite a spell. For that matter, he hadn't even thrown a snowball at her lately. There'd been a dark cloud over Wraight, it seemed, these last few weeks. He'd been spending more and more time with Lundy and Smith, and they were not the best kind of friends to have. Those boys were trouble.

She wondered if maybe Lundy wasn't the one who'd written that awful message on the school wall. Of course, Lizette hadn't said anything to Miz Christy. She didn't exactly have any proof. And Lundy wasn't the kind of boy you wanted to tangle with, that was for sure.

Slowly Lizette turned around again. Wraight was still staring at her. She smiled, and this time, she thought maybe—just maybe—she saw him smile back. But when Lundy whispered something to Wraight, his smile vanished.

Lizette picked up her chalk and made another heart. *L.H.* + , she wrote.

She left the rest of the heart empty.

Four

That afternoon, Christy walked to the Spencers' cabin. The Spencer children—John, Zady, Clara, and Lulu—went with her. Lizette Holcombe came along too. As official Junior Teachers, John and Lizette were anxious to talk about ways they could help the younger students. As she listened to their discussion, Christy felt very pleased. Her Junior Teacher idea was obviously going to be a big success.

As they walked through the sun-dappled woods, filled with the clean scent of pine and balsam, Christy could almost forget the ugly message on the schoolhouse. Even with the help of her students, it had taken most of the noon recess to scrub off the messy letters.

The Spencers' cabin came into view at the top of a ridge. Christy thought back to the first time she'd met the Spencer family. When no one had been at the train station to greet her, Christy had decided to set off on the seven-mile journey to the mission with Mr. Pentland as he delivered the mail. They'd stopped at the Spencers' cabin to warm themselves. But almost as soon as they'd sat down before the fire, a man named Bob Allen had been carried into the cabin on a homemade stretcher. Mr. Allen had been on his way to meet Christy at the station when a tree had fallen on his head. He was very badly hurt.

Before long, the local doctor, Neil MacNeill, had arrived to perform risky brain surgery right there in the Spencers' simple cabin. Christy had actually assisted the doctor during the operation. The doctor was a big handsome man, if a little gruff. Christy had been amazed at his skill, not to mention his ability to remain calm under tremendous pressure.

Fortunately, Bob had survived. But she had felt terribly guilty about his accident—after all, he'd been on his way to meet her when it had happened.

During the anxious moments before and after the operation, Fairlight Spencer had offered Christy a gentle voice and a kind smile. She was graceful woman, with delicate features and lovely eyes. Somehow she didn't seem to belong in that primitive cabin, tucked far away in the woods. Christy had liked Fairlight instantly, and she had the feeling they would grow to be good friends.

Jeb Spencer, Fairlight's husband, was in the yard, chopping wood. When he heard the children coming, he set his ax down and opened his arms to hug Lulu, his six-year-old daughter, who was running to greet him.

Two of the dogs raced over to John, yapping eagerly.

"And how was school today, you rascal?" Jeb asked Lulu. Jeb had deep-set blue eyes and a red beard. The front of his hat was pinned up with a long thorn. A sprig of balsam stuck out from the hat band like a feather. In spite of his ragged clothing, there was something dashing about him.

"Pa, we brought Teacher home with us!" Lulu cried proudly.

"So I see," Jeb said. He removed his hat and gave Christy a little bow. "Howdy-do, Miz Christy. Fairlight's been so excited about your comin', she ain't sat still all day long."

Fairlight was waiting at the door of the cabin. Little Guy, a chubby-faced toddler, clutched at her worn calico skirt. "I'm so glad you come, Miz Christy," Fairlight said, her face glowing. "I was half afraid you wouldn't. Jeb's right. I've been so all-fired excited, I've been buzzin' around this cabin like a hungry bee a-huntin' for honey."

Christy laughed. "Of course I came, Fairlight. I've been looking forward to starting our lessons. I'm just sorry we couldn't start sooner. It's taken me a while to get settled in."

"With all those young'uns to teach, I should say so!" Fairlight exclaimed. "Come on in. You children, too, but mind your manners. There's gingerbread I made fresh, but don't be eatin' it all. We have company."

The Spencer cabin was just two rooms: a kitchen area and a main room that served as dining room, living room, and bedroom. The floor was bare. Clothes and a worn saddle hung off pegs on the wall. Across an elk-horn rack rested a long-barreled rifle. A narrow ladder led to a hole in the ceiling where a sleeping loft was located.

The first time Christy had seen this cabin, she'd been shocked at the primitive conditions. The Spencers had no running water, no phone, and no electricity. Stepping into their home was almost like stepping into another century, back to the days of the American frontier.

But since then, Christy had visited some of the other cabins in the area. Now she saw how much Fairlight had done to make this simple home special. She'd made the cabin warm and inviting by adding little touches of beauty. The rickety table by the fire, for example, was covered by a worn piece of delicately embroidered fabric. A chipped ceramic bowl sat on top of the table. Fairlight had carefully arranged sprigs of pine and balsam in it, then added the first delicate crocuses of the spring for a bit of color. Next to the bowl rested a plate piled high with gingerbread, still warm.

Christy sat down at the table. On the floor beside her she placed the box of teaching materials she'd brought along. Little Guy climbed onto her lap. He seemed to be fascinated, like all the children, with her soft red sweater.

She accepted a piece of gingerbread from Fairlight. Giving half of it to Little Guy, she took a bite of the spicy bread. "Fairlight, this is wonderful," she exclaimed.

John grabbed two pieces of gingerbread. When Fairlight sent him a warning look, he quickly said, "One's for Lizette."

"What are those fancy things you two are wearing?" Fairlight asked, pointing to John's badge.

"We're Junior Teachers," John said proudly. "Me and Lizette and Rob Allen. We get to help Miz Christy with the young'uns."

"Well, that's mighty impressive," Fairlight said, winking at Christy. "I'm proud of you, John. And just to give you a little extra practice, you can keep an eye on Lulu and Little Guy while Miz Christy and me are a-studyin'."

John groaned.

"We don't mind," Lizette said with a grin. "Come on, Little Guy." She reached for the toddler and lifted him off Christy's lap. As they passed the fireplace, Lizette's gaze fell on the dulcimer that belonged to Jeb. "John," she said, "did you ever think of learnin' to play the dulcimer like your pa does?"

John shrugged. "Naw. Pa plays enough for all of us. You know how he loves his ballad singin'."

"Wraight plays," Lizette said.

"So?" John asked.

"So . . . nothin'. Have you ever heard him?" Christy noticed her eyes had a faraway look in them.

"Nope. Don't want to, neither. Besides, I think Wraight Holt has a voice like a bullfrog with the sniffles."

Lizette smiled wistfully. "You know that ain't so. When that boy takes a notion to sing, he's got more music in him than a tree full of birds."

"What are we talking about Wraight for, anyways?" John demanded. He glanced at Christy and his mother, then lowered his voice a bit. "He's trouble."

"No, he ain't," Lizette said.

"Well, he and Lundy and Smith are friends. And those other two ain't exactly angels. Look at what happened today at school. And yesterday."

"That don't mean Wraight had anything to—"

"Come on," John said gruffly. "We've got work to do."

Christy and Fairlight watched John and Lizette head over to the far corner of the room. Fairlight leaned close to Christy. "Near as I can figure, John's got a real hankerin' for Lizette. Lately, he's been walkin' around all moony eyed." She lowered her voice. "But I have a feelin' Lizette don't feel the same way about John. I'm just guessin', mind you, but I think she's got her heart set on Wraight Holt."

Christy nodded. "It does sound that way, doesn't it?"

"What was John talkin' about?" Fairlight asked, reaching

for a piece of gingerbread. "Did somethin' happen at the school?"

"Someone wrote 'Get away, Teacher' on the side of the schoolhouse," Christy said with a sigh. "Not only that, they nailed the front door shut."

Fairlight blinked in disbelief. "Who done it, do you figure?"

"I wish I knew. Naturally, I suspect Lundy Taylor. But I don't have any proof. And I thought I saw Zach Holt running from the school . . ."

"Zach's such a good boy," Fairlight said. "I reckon it wasn't him, unless one of the big boys put him up to it."

"Well, whoever it was, he wasn't a good speller." Christy smiled. "And speaking of spelling, we have more important things to be talking about. Shall we start?"

"I can't wait," Fairlight said. Her eyes were wide with excitement.

Christy opened the box she'd brought. Inside lay a copy of the alphabet printed in large, clear letters; a Bible; a fresh ruled pad; and some pictures Christy had cut out from old magazines. Some were of landscapes. Others were figures of men, women, and children pasted onto cardboard bases so they could be stood upright, the way Christy used to do with paper dolls when she was a little girl. She was hoping to find a new and interesting way to teach Fairlight. She didn't want to use the same simple books she used for children beginning to read—the ones that began with sentences like "The rat ran from the cat."

Christy picked up the Bible. "There are lots and lots of words in this book."

"How soon will I be able to read it, Miz Christy?"

"In no time. And I'll tell you why. All the words in this book use only twenty-six English letters." She pointed to the alphabet. "After you've learned how to put the letters together, then, with some practice, you'll be able to read."

Fairlight's eyes shone. "I'd like that the best in the world."

After they had read through the alphabet twice, Fairlight began studying the letters with such concentration that she seemed to forget Christy was even there. After a while, she looked up. "Think I've got it," she announced. "A—B—C—D . . ." She went all the way through the alphabet, only making one mistake.

John and Lizette applauded. "Ma, that was wonderful!" John exclaimed.

"Isn't she the smartest ma in the whole wide world, Miz Christy?" cried twelve-year-old Clara, who was playing by the fire with her younger sister, Zady.

"Fairlight, I can tell you are going to be a wonderful student," Christy said. She felt almost as excited as Fairlight clearly was. She propped up one of the background pictures of a landscape drenched in sunlight. "Now, Fairlight, you pick out one of the paper people from this pile."

Fairlight selected a well-dressed young man and stood him up before the landscape. Christy taught her the word *man*, and Fairlight eagerly practiced saying it and forming the letters. Soon they'd moved on to *tree, sun, grass, sky*, and *light*. Before long, Fairlight had mastered ten words.

Christy opened the Bible to the first chapter of Genesis. "Now, Fairlight, look at this," she said. "The words on this page are just ideas marching along. Like this one: 'And God said, Let there be light.'"

"*L-i-g-h-t*," Fairlight spelled out. "There it is! 'Light'! Just like in my own name. I see it!" She turned to Clara and Zady. "Look, girls. *L-i-g-h-t*, 'light.'"

Christy couldn't help beaming. It was such a thrill to be able to open up a whole new world of reading to someone like Fairlight, who was so grateful for the chance to learn.

"Before long, you'll be reading the Bible to the children," Christy said. "I must say, Fairlight, you're a joy to teach."

Zady pulled on Christy's sleeve. "How about us, Teacher?" she asked, her dark eyes wide. "Are we joys too?"

"You are a joy to teach too," Christy said, patting Zady on the head. "All my students are."

"Even Wraight and Lundy and Smith?" John asked from the corner.

"Even them," Christy said. Although the truth was there had been many days when she'd wished the older boys weren't at school trying her patience and testing her will.

Fairlight turned toward the only window. "What was that?" she asked, frowning.

"What?" Christy asked.

"Thought I heard somethin' at the window."

"Probably just Pa," John said, standing. "But I'll go check."

Outside the window, the shadows had grown long. Already the sun was vanishing behind the mountains. "I should get going," Christy said. "Miss Ida frets so if I'm late for dinner."

"John'll walk you," Fairlight said.

Christy shook her head. "Oh, there's no need."

"I'll walk with you partway, Miz Christy," Lizette volunteered. "Time for me to get goin', anyhow."

"John'll walk you both," Fairlight insisted.

"All right, then," Christy said, recalling her promise to David that morning.

John appeared in the doorway. "Ain't nothin', Ma," he reported. "Pa stackin' logs, most likely. He says he didn't see or hear nothin'."

"Probably just my ears playin' tricks on me," Fairlight said. "John, I want you to walk Miz Christy and Lizette on home. It's gettin' on toward dark, and I'm afraid I took up way too much time with my schoolin'."

"Don't be silly, Fairlight," Christy assured her. "I enjoyed every minute. In fact, I can't wait for us to get together again for another lesson. I'll leave that box of materials for you to work on."

"Meantime, maybe I can get me some help from my very own Junior Teacher," Fairlight said, giving John a hug.

John blushed, glancing over at Lizette. "We'd best get goin'," he said, pulling out of his mother's grasp.

"Thank you again, Miz Christy. I'm goin' to practice my letters till I know 'em backwards and forwards and inside out."

After Christy said goodbye to the children and to Jeb, she and Lizette and John set out along the rough path toward the mission. They took a slight detour that led to Lizette's cabin. When Lizette was safely inside, John and Christy resumed their walk to the mission.

After a few minutes of silence, John turned to Christy. "Have you ever been . . ."

"Ever been what, John?"

"You know." He picked up the pace. "You know, sweet on somebody?"

Christy hurried to catch up. "Well, once or twice, I suppose."

"Lizette says the preacher's sweet on you."

"Oh, she does, does she?"

John gave a terse nod. "S'posin' the preacher were sweet on you, but you weren't sweet on him?"

Christy felt herself blushing. She wasn't "sweet on" David, exactly. After all, she'd only known him a little while. But she had to admit she did look forward to his sly smiles and silly jokes.

"Miz Christy?"

Christy cleared her throat. "All right, then. Let's suppose. As long as you understand we're just supposing."

"Well, s'posin'—" Suddenly John stopped in his tracks. "You hear somethin'?"

Christy paused, straining to hear. "No."

"Bushes cracklin'."

"No, I don't hear anything." Christy glanced over her shoulder. The trees cast long, black shadows. The edges of the sky were tinged with pink, but the sun had vanished.

"Hearin' things, I guess. Sorry."

"So, John, you were saying?" Christy asked as they started walking again.

"Oh. That. I guess I was just wonderin' if there's a way to get a girl to be sweet on you when maybe she ain't."

"That's a good question. I suppose you should just be the person you really are, John. And if Liz—I mean, this girl— isn't the right one for you, trust me, someone else will come along who sees how special you really are."

John gave a small, hopeful smile. "You reckon?"

"I'm sure of it."

After a few more minutes, they reached the last ridge before the mission. The first stars had begun to glimmer.

"You go on home, now, John," Christy said. "If you head back now, you might not miss dinner."

"No'm. I promised I'd take you all the way."

"John," Christy said firmly. "I insist. Otherwise I'll have to worry about you."

John hesitated. "I don't mind, Miz Christy—"

"But I do. The mission is just over the next ridge, and I don't want you going home in complete darkness." She put her hands on her hips. "Now, go home. That's an order. After all, you may be a Junior Teacher. But I'm the Senior Teacher."

John laughed. "All right then. You take care to go straight over the ridge so you don't get sidetracked. The path is hard to follow when it gets this dark." He started to turn, then hesitated. "Miz Christy?"

"Yes, John?"

"Thanks for the . . . uh, the advice."

"Anytime."

Christy smiled as she started up the crude path. John was a nice boy. She wondered why Lizette was interested in Wraight—if she really was. Well, love was funny that way. Maybe Lizette saw something in Wraight that Christy couldn't see.

She climbed up the path, taking careful steps because of the patches of snow and mud. After a while, the path seemed to disappear in the twilight gloom. Hadn't it been better marked? The hill was steeper than she'd remembered it too.

She stopped. Had she lost the trail, just as John had warned her not to do? It had been here a minute ago—

Behind her, something cracked. It was the distinct, loud crunch of a dry stick breaking.

An animal, Christy told herself. She turned, straining her

eyes to see if she could make out anything. John had long since vanished. She saw no animals. Nothing. In the near darkness, the trees blended into one another, forming a lacy black curtain. She gazed back toward the top of the ridge. Above her, a stand of pines lurked like a group of menacing giants.

Hoo-hoo-oo-hoo-hoo.

Christy started. It was an owl, that much she knew. She wasn't such a "city gal" that she'd never heard an owl before. But it seemed to be coming from deep in the bushes, just a few yards to her left. Shouldn't any self-respecting owl be up in a tree?

You're almost home, Christy, she told herself. *Relax.*

It was just like Fairlight had said—her ears were playing tricks on her.

Christy quickened her pace, but the snow was hard and icy in spots. She'd only gained a few feet when she slipped and fell. She landed on the cold ground with a thud. As she struggled to untangle her long skirts, a deep, horrifying howling noise seemed to fill the whole woods. It was the cry of a wolf, so close it might have been just inches away.

Christy froze in place. Her heart galloped in her chest. If he saw her move, he might attack.

The howl came again, a long, sad wail. It was close, too close. She was sure she could hear the wild, dangerous animal breathing.

Whatever you do, she told herself, *don't move.*

On the other hand, she couldn't sit here all night in the cold, could she? They'd find her here tomorrow, stiff as a statue, with a look of terror permanently frozen on her face.

No, that was too awful to think about. One way or another, she had to take her chances.

Christy stumbled slowly to her feet. There was no point in looking for the path now. She'd just aim for the top of the ridge, where the dark blue sky glistened with a dusting of stars. She couldn't run up the steep, bramble-covered hill, even if she'd wanted to. Instead she grabbed at limbs and bushes wherever she could, pulling herself toward the top.

She held her breath as she made her way past the spot where she'd imagined the wolf—or whatever the source of that horrible howl—was hiding. She tried to be quiet, but every step meant the sound of cracking branches or crunching snow.

Nothing happened. No knife-toothed creature leapt from the darkness to tear at her throat. The only sound was the gentle creak and moan of an old tree nearby, fighting the wind.

See? Christy told herself. *You let your imagination get the better of you. Now, relax. You've lost the path, but once you reach the top of the ridge, the mission will be in view. In a few more minutes, you'll be sitting at the dinner table, laughing about your imaginary "wolf."*

Step, grab. Step, grab. It was slow going, but she was almost to the top. The trees had grown so thick that she had to squeeze between some of them. The smell of pines perfumed the night air. Their needles made a soft, swishing noise, like whispering voices. The bare branches of other trees clicked and cracked, but Christy told herself it was just the wind.

Near the top of the ridge, the trees thinned out a bit. Christy was panting. She paused to lean against a tall pine. "You're almost there," she said aloud. "Just a few more—"

Suddenly, she heard something falling from the tree. Christy screamed as it glanced off her shoulder before landing on the ground. Whatever it was, it was wet and soft and small. Swallowing back her fear, Christy knelt.

It was a rat, a dead one. Starlight shone in its glassy eyes. Christy shuddered and backed away. She stared up into the pine tree.

Just then, a shadowy figure leapt out from behind a nearby tree, and once again, with all her might, Christy screamed.

Five

THE FIGURE MOVED CLOSER AND CLOSER.

Christy backed against the pine. Her heart hammered in her chest. Her fists were clenched.

"Miz Christy, don't be scared. It's me."

Christy blinked. She didn't recognize the boy's voice. But she did recognize the red cap.

"Zach Holt?" she asked in a trembling voice. "Is that you, Zach?"

The little boy came close and extended his hand. Even in near darkness, she could see that his forehead was beaded with sweat. Pine needles stuck to his ragged, patched coat. A small stick was caught on his cap.

"Zach, what are you doing here? You weren't . . . following me, were you?"

"Me?" Zach cried. "No'm. Not me. I was just—" He hesitated. "I was just out huntin' possum."

"With your bare hands?"

Zach swallowed. "It's a special trick my pa taught me," he said quickly. "You corner 'em, and then when they play possum—you know, all curled up like they's dead—you whomp 'em on the head with a stick."

"I see." Christy crossed her arms over her chest. Now that her fear was fading, she was left with far too many questions. "I heard noises before," she said. "Branches cracking, that sort of thing. It sounded like somebody was following me."

With great care, Zach examined some pine needles on his coat.

"And I heard a wolf. At least, I thought it was a wolf."

"Coulda been." Zach nodded. "There's lots of wolves around these here parts. They get real mean this time of year. Hungry too."

Christy nudged the dead rat on the ground with her toe. "Are there lots of tree rats in the area too?"

Zach gulped. "Tree rats? Ain't never heard of no tree rats, ma'am."

"I haven't, either. So how do you explain this one? It fell out of this pine tree. And nearly scared me to death, I might add."

Zach glanced up quickly at the upper branches of the tree, then met Christy's eyes. "Just can't mortally explain it, Miz Christy."

Christy stared up at the tree. She saw nothing but a blur of dark branches.

"Could be that's not a ground rat, factually speaking," Zach suggested. "Could be one of them there flyin' rats."

"Ah. Those must be very rare. I've never heard of them."

"Well, you're from the city. Ain't no flyin' rats in the city. They hate cars and such."

"I see."

"You heard of flyin' squirrels?"

"Yes. Now that you mention it, I believe I have." Christy tried not to smile. She was torn between her anger at having been scared and her amusement at Zach's desperate attempt to explain the rat.

"Flyin' rats is the same thing. Only instead of big fuzzy tails, they got scrawny ones."

"Well, then. Thank you for clearing that up, Zach."

He pointed to the top of the ridge. "If'n you like, I could walk you the rest of the way home."

"Actually, I'm more worried about you getting home, safe and sound."

"Oh, don't fret about me none. I got company—" Zach swallowed hard. "What I mean to say is I got me the stars and the trees for company. I know these woods like the back of my own hand, anyways."

"I'd be pleased to have you as an escort, then, Zach," Christy said.

They climbed in silence. At last they reached the top of the ridge. Below them, the mission house was a welcome sight. Yellow light glowed in the windows, and Christy could just make out the figure of Miss Ida inside, bustling to and fro.

Christy brushed the snow off a fallen log and sat down. She motioned for Zach to join her there. "I'd like to rest up, Zach, before I go the rest of the way. Maybe you could keep me company for a moment."

"Well . . ." Zach sat down, looking very uncomfortable. "My pa gets ornery if'n I'm out too long. I oughta be gettin' on. That is, if'n you don't need me to es-squirt you the rest of the way."

"Escort." Christy smiled. "Are you close to your pa, Zach?"

"Close?"

"You know. Do you two like to talk? Go hunting and fishing together, that sort of thing?"

"Not a whole heap. He talks some, I s'pose." Zach kicked at a stone. "Pa's got kind of a mean streak in him, when he gets to drinkin' moonshine."

Christy nodded. Miss Alice had told her that illegal liquor was a big problem here in the mountains.

"That must be hard for you when he gets like that," she said gently.

"Ain't so hard. I'm used to it. Wraight, he—" Zach stopped himself.

"What, Zach?"

"Nothin'. It's just . . . now and again, he gets riled up somethin' fierce about Pa. Wraight's got a temper, see, and so does Pa." He gave a little shrug. "'Course it's not real feudin', mind you. Not like the Taylors and the Allens or nothin'."

"I've heard that the Taylor and Allen families have been fighting each other for a long, long time," Christy said. "Why are they still fighting, do you think?"

Zach looked at her in confusion, as if he couldn't understand why she'd even bother asking. "Way back when, the Taylors and Allens got to shootin' each other, and they ain't never stopped. Could be over moonshinin'." He shrugged. "Could be over nothin'."

Once again Christy felt a deep sadness for mountain children like Zach. They were so used to hate and fighting and killing. It wasn't fair. They grew up far too fast.

"Zach," she asked casually, "do you like Lundy?"

"He's all right enough, I s'pose."

"But you're friends with him, aren't you?"

"I'm too little. Wraight's his friend more'n I am."

Christy stared up at the starry sky. "I guess Lundy can be kind of a bully, can't he?"

Zach answered with a small nod.

"I can see how it might be hard for someone—especially someone smaller—to say no to Lundy."

"Right hard," Zach agreed.

Christy sighed. This was tougher than she'd thought it would be. She was almost certain that Lundy was putting Zach up to these pranks. But could she ever get the little boy to admit it, as long as he was so afraid of Lundy?

She decided to try the direct approach. "Zach, did Lundy make you follow me this evening, to try to scare me?"

"No'm," Zach said, leaping off the log. "Don't be gettin' Lundy all mixed up in this. It'll just make things worse!"

"Zach, what are you talking about?"

"I got to go, Miz Christy. My pa and all. Will you be all right the rest of the way over to the mission?"

"Of course I will. And thank you, Zach, for taking me this far."

With an awkward tip of his little red cap, Zach slipped into the trees and vanished.

⟶

The next day at school, Christy didn't say anything to Zach about the incident in the woods. She noticed that he seemed even quieter than usual. Wraight and Lundy, on the other hand, were especially bad tempered and rude. Twice she'd had to scold them during reading lessons.

It had been a frustrating day, even with the help of her new Junior Teachers. When Lizette had tried to help Wraight with his spelling, he'd snapped at her so gruffly that she'd practically cried. Christy was glad when the school day finally ended. As she stood in the doorway, saying goodbye to the children, she was surprised to see Mr. Pentland appear at the top of the ridge.

"Back so soon?" Christy called.

"Not just me," Mr. Pentland yelled back. He jerked his thumb back toward the woods. "Got some delivery folks a-comin' too. Mighty big load."

"Oh, that's wonderful!" Christy exclaimed. "Donations for the mission?"

"Yep. All of it's for the mission, near as I can tell. Been piling up at the train station for a while now."

Soon a big wagon, pulled by two pairs of strong oxen, lumbered into the schoolyard. It was piled high with crates and boxes. Some were covered with a large tarp. Christy ran to greet the procession. So her letter-writing campaign had worked, after all. What would David and Miss Alice say when they saw how well her plan had worked?

Most of the children, who'd been about to head home, stayed to watch as the two delivery men began unloading large boxes. Only Zach, Lundy, Wraight, and Smith hung back on the porch, as sullen and watchful as ever.

"My, it's Christmas in March!" David exclaimed, rushing over to help the delivery men. "Are you sure they're in the right place, Mr. Pentland?"

"Yep. Took two days to get here over those rutted roads. But they figured better now than when the spring thaw comes and the mud with it. It's all for the mission. Oh, 'ceptin' this package for you, Miz Christy." Mr. Pentland reached into his bag and handed her a small package. It was wrapped in brown paper and tied with a string. "Mighty big week for deliveries."

The careful handwriting on the package told Christy it was from her mother.

"Ain't you goin' to open it, Teacher?" Ruby Mae asked.

"I'll save it for later," Christy said. "We've got enough to open, don't you think?"

David borrowed a hammer from one of the delivery men and began to open a large wooden crate. "This says 'To Miss Christy Rudd Huddleston,'" David said. "'From the Martin Textile Company in Charlotte, North Carolina.'" He grinned at her. "You have connections in Charlotte?"

"Well, not exactly," Christy said. "It's a long story."

The top of the crate popped off.

"Blankets!" Ruby Mae cried. She and Bessie began pulling out the fresh wool blankets one by one.

David opened another crate from the same company, this one filled with pillows.

One by one, he revealed the contents of the other crates. Each time, the children gathered around, gasping in surprise at the bounty inside. Christy beamed as she watched the donations pile up. All of it was so desperately needed—sheets, towels, rugs, cleaning supplies, medicine. And all of it was the result of Christy's letter-writing campaign. The exception was two barrels of secondhand clothing sent by her mother's church. The Bell Company had even come through with a large donation of telephone wire and a telephone.

David stared at the wire, frowning in disbelief. "And how exactly am I going to hook up telephone lines?" he asked.

"Well, you built an entire schoolhouse, didn't you?"

Christy said with a wink. "How hard will it be to install one little telephone?"

"It has to be connected up, you know. Two ends, something to carry the voice."

"A telephone," Ruby Mae exclaimed. "Wouldn't that just be the most all-fired amazin' thing Cutter Gap ever seen? How long will it take you to hook it up, Preacher?"

David rolled his eyes. "I wouldn't hold your breath, Ruby Mae. It may be a very long wait, in spite of your teacher's confidence in me."

"But David—" Christy began, stinging a little from the sarcasm in his voice. After all, she'd gone to a lot of trouble to get the telephone equipment. Couldn't he at least show a little gratitude?

"Well, well. This is quite a sight," Miss Alice called from her cabin porch. But the look on her face was not exactly what Christy had hoped to see. She'd expected Miss Alice to be as thrilled as she was about the donations. Instead, her mentor looked almost annoyed.

"Looky here, Miss Alice," Little Burl said, running to grab her hand as she approached. "There's pillows in that there crate, soft as can be."

"So I see."

Miss Alice met Christy's eyes. Now Christy was certain of it. Her heart sank a little. Miss Alice was not pleased.

David held up the wire. "Christy apparently thinks that with my magical skills, I'll be able to string up a telephone wire. She seems to have forgotten that the wire has to go over two mountains, not to mention a river."

Just then, John cried out. "Ooo-wee! Will you look at this!"

He and Creed had managed to open a large cardboard box. Christy recognized the printing on the top of the box. It was from a textbook supplier she'd written. Could it be?

John held up a brand-new history textbook. "Real, live books!" he cried. "Have you ever seen anythin' so all-fired pretty?"

Christy joined the boys. The other children crowded close. It was more than she'd ever dreamed possible—maps, books, even a globe, and an American flag.

"Oh, Miss Alice," Christy cried. "Isn't it wonderful?"

"I'm glad, for the sake of the children," Miss Alice said quietly, "but I do think we need to have a talk, Christy."

Before Christy could respond, Little Burl grabbed her arm. "Teacher," he said urgently, "what's under the big blanket over yonder on the wagon? Those are the biggest boxes I ever did see!"

Christy was almost afraid to ask. Judging from Miss Alice's stern look, she had made some terrible mistake. Still, she had no choice but to ask.

"Mr. Pentland," she said, "what's under the tarp? More boxes? Or maybe mattresses?"

"No'm. I reckon you remember how I told you somethin' was a-comin' that could make noise?" He signaled to the two delivery men, who yanked the tarp free.

Everyone gasped, but no one was more stunned than Christy.

A beautiful, brand-new, gleaming, grand piano sat on its side in the wagon.

"Oh, my!" Christy said, her hand to her mouth.

"Oh, my, indeed," said Miss Alice.

"Mercy, Teacher!" whispered Creed. "What is it?"

"It's a piano, Creed. A concert grand piano. It makes beautiful music."

Even Lundy and his friends ran over, staring at the piano in awe. Wraight reached out and touched the shiny black piano bench, his jaw slightly ajar.

"Ain't it just purty?" Ruby Mae said to Wraight.

He gave a small nod, his fingers lingering on the smooth wood.

Christy turned to Miss Alice and David. "Well," she said a little sheepishly, "surprise!"

David slowly shook his head. He could not seem to find the right words. "Christy," he said at last, "that may be the understatement of the year."

Six

But I thought you'd be pleased," Christy said after dinner that night. She was sitting at the dining room table with David, Miss Alice, and Miss Ida. Ruby Mae worked in the kitchen, cleaning up the dishes.

The boxes of donations sat in the living room, along with the grand piano. It had taken David, Mr. Pentland, and the two delivery men several frustrating hours to get it into the mission house.

Miss Ida pursed her lips. "Miss Alice doesn't like begging," she said primly.

"But I didn't beg, exactly," Christy said lamely. "I just wrote a nice letter to some companies. I explained the mission's desperate need for supplies. And I told them about the children. That's all."

"Now's the time for me to explain the mission's philosophy of fundraising," Miss Alice said. She paused to pour a fresh cup of tea from a steaming pot. "We believe that only one reason is good enough for a person to give: because that person, without pressure, freely chooses to make the gift.

Money pried out of people won't be blessed for the work we need to do, anyway. Donations must come from the heart."

Christy hung her head. "I understand. At least, I think I do."

"As much as we need those supplies, you risked putting the mission in a bad light, Christy," Miss Alice continued. "I honestly don't think going ahead on your own like this was even good teamwork."

Christy nodded. She thought of many explanations for her behavior, but she knew Miss Alice was right. "I guess sometimes I do go running off on my own," she admitted.

"Independence can be a good thing," Miss Alice said. "But you've only been here a brief time. Before you go changing the world, take things a little more slowly, and consult David and me. Sometimes it's hard to see the whole picture. For example, these donations are going to cause some unintended problems."

"But how could they? The mission desperately needs everything that was sent." Christy paused. David was gazing at the piano, grinning widely. "With the possible exception of the grand piano," she added.

"The thing is, Christy, we can't simply give these items away to the mountain people." Miss Alice sat back in her chair. "There's a strong mountain code, you see. No one wants to owe anyone for anything. These people don't respect anyone who can't earn his own way."

"But all the clothes!" Christy cried. "We can't just let them sit there in the barrels, untouched. There are lots of shoes in good condition, Miss Alice. You know how badly the children need shoes."

"You're right. But do you see my point?" Miss Alice asked gently. "You need to understand the mountain people before you can help them. Your intentions were good. But the result was not precisely what you'd hoped. If you simply give away all these items, then people will feel like the few things they've worked so hard for are worth less. We must always remember that this mission represents a change for Cutter Gap. We hope it will be a change for the better. But change can be frightening too. And frightened people can become angry people."

For a moment, everyone sat quietly, contemplating the boxes and barrels stacked high in the parlor.

Suddenly, David snapped his fingers. "I have an idea!" he exclaimed. "Suppose we sell the clothes? Priced very low, of course. We could set up a little store. Charge something like seventy-five cents for a good suit, five cents for a vest. That sort of thing."

"That's a wonderful idea," Christy said, relieved that the donations might not have to go to waste. "And maybe we could accept vegetables or other things as payment instead of money. That way, all the mountain people would have a chance to get what they need, no matter how poor they are."

"I think that's a fine solution to a tricky problem," Miss Alice pronounced.

Ruby Mae came in, drying her hands on a dish towel. "I been meanin' to ask you," she said. "Are we goin' to have some kind of jollification, now that we have that giant piano thing right there in the middle of the parlor, just a-waitin' for some playin'?"

"Another fine idea!" Miss Alice said. "How about an open house?"

"Ruby Mae, you're brilliant," David said. "We could have a party here, with music and dancing, and invite everyone from Cutter Gap. Jeb can play his dulcimer, and I'll play my ukulele."

"I play a little piano," Christy said. "Not very well, but I could give it a try."

"Wonderful," said Miss Alice. "How about Saturday night? Ruby Mae, you spread the word."

"I'll get right on that, Miz Alice," Ruby Mae said excitedly. "Be tickled to death to help out."

"With Ruby Mae on the job, everyone in Cutter Gap will know about it within an hour," David teased.

Ruby Mae rolled her eyes, then slapped at David playfully with the dish towel.

Miss Alice leaned over to Miss Ida, whose brow was creased with a deep frown. "What's wrong, Miss Ida?"

"I was just thinking about what a mess an open house like that will make!" Miss Ida sighed. "I'll be cleaning up for a month or more."

"Don't worry, Miss Ida," Christy said. "I'll get the children to help."

Miss Ida seemed to relax a little.

"Don't you fret none, Miss Ida," Ruby Mae said, patting her on the shoulder. "Last jollification I went to, over at the Holcombes', it weren't hardly any mess at all." She shrugged. "Unless, of course, you count that broken window. Or when the kitchen caught on fire . . ."

Miss Ida groaned, dropping her head into her hands.

Christy winked at Ruby Mae. "You've probably reassured Miss Ida enough for one evening, Ruby Mae."

"Well, now," David said to Christy. "It seems everything worked out for the best. We've found a way to deal with all these donations, and we even managed to get that piano inside. One of these days, I may even figure out how to hook up that telephone of yours."

"Still, I'm sorry about all this," Christy said. "I only meant to help, but I can see now that I went a little too fast." She sighed. "Sometimes I wonder if I'll ever really understand these people. Take last night, when I thought I was being chased on my way home from the Spencers' cabin. I ran into Zach Holt, but when I tried to question him—"

"Did you just say 'when I thought I was being chased'?" David interrupted. "What are you talking about? I thought John Spencer walked you home."

"He did. And it's nothing, really, David," Christy said with a wave of her hand. "That's why I didn't mention it yesterday when I got home. I heard some noises, a dead rat dropped out of a pine tree—"

"A what?" David exclaimed.

"I'm sure it was just more of the same. Another prank, that's all. The odd thing was that Zach suddenly appeared, out of nowhere. But try as I might, I couldn't get him to admit that Lundy has been putting him up to these things. And I'm sure that's what's going on."

"I don't like this, not at all," David said. "This is getting out of hand."

Miss Alice shook her head. "One thing's clear, anyway. That message on the school is not going to be the end of these pranks."

"You've got to be more careful, Christy," David said sternly.

"I will, I promise—"

"No, I don't think you understand. This is just like the situation with the donations. You think you understand these people, but you don't—not yet. They can be violent. Very violent. People in Cutter Gap have been shot for no reason."

"But if this prankster is just one of the children . . ." Christy's voice trailed off. "I can't believe any of them would be capable of real violence."

"Don't be too sure," Miss Ida warned.

"It can't hurt to be careful, Christy," Miss Alice said. "To begin with, you're not completely sure that one of the children is responsible. Until we can put a stop to this, I think you should stay close to the mission for a while, and be very careful."

"I understand," Christy said. "But it sure seems to me like you're worrying over nothing."

Miss Alice seemed surprised by Christy's reaction. "Don't forget what I told you. In these mountains, anything new and strange poses a threat. And here we have a new schoolhouse, a new starry-eyed teacher, and now, new books. For some, that may add up to a threat to the only way of life they've ever known. Don't forget all the mischief Granny O'Teale was able to make when she decided you were cursed."

Christy gave a wry laugh. "How could I? Still, I hate to think one of the children feels that way." She pushed back her chair and stood. "Did you ever have one of those days when you felt like you couldn't do anything right?"

"Don't be silly," Miss Alice said, reaching over to pat Christy's arm. "You're doing so much right. You've made great strides with the children already. And I know you're going to do much more, with time."

"That will only be possible if they'll let me."

A smile tugged at the corners of Miss Alice's mouth. "Remember Matthew 19:26, Christy: 'With God all things are possible.'"

⌐_⌐

Up in her room, Christy settled on her bed and carefully opened the package Mr. Pentland had brought her today. Inside was a note written in her mother's careful handwriting and a gift, about the size of a book, wrapped in pretty blue tissue paper. Carefully, Christy tore off the paper. She wanted to save as much as she could. Perhaps she could use it for an art project at school.

Inside, to her surprise, was a brand-new leather-covered diary and a new fountain pen. Christy had told her mother how she'd given her old diary away to Ruby Mae after Christy had caught her snooping in it. Christy had torn out the few pages where she'd written about her journey to Cutter Gap. The rest of the diary had been untouched, and Ruby had been thrilled at the idea of having a private place all her own where she could write down her thoughts and dreams. As hard as it had been to part with the diary, Christy had never regretted giving it away.

Now, here was her chance to start fresh. Something told her it was important to record everything that happened to her here at the mission. She knew she was on an important adventure, even if she had no idea how it would all unfold.

Christy opened to the first page. On it, her mother had written:

February 21, 1912
For my lovely and brave daughter, to record all her
adventures.

All my love,
Mother

A hot lump formed in Christy's throat. There were many days when she missed her parents and her brother, George, so much that it felt like she could hardly bear it.

Even though her parents had at first argued against her coming here, once Christy had made up her mind to teach in Cutter Gap, they had been completely supportive. She traced her fingers over her mother's message. Christy could almost hear her talking to the women's group at the church about her daughter's wonderful work in the mountains. She could imagine her as she'd carefully folded each sweater and dress into the donation barrels that had arrived today.

But was Christy's work here so amazing? Sometimes she wondered. Obviously, she had disappointed Miss Alice today. And she'd angered someone enough to cause a string of angry pranks.

Christy reached for the pen and began to write.

Wednesday, March 13, 1912
My first entry in my new diary. As I continue my
adventures in Cutter Gap, I pray that I won't let down
my parents, Miss Alice, David, or the children. And most
important, perhaps, I pray I won't let myself down.
I can be far too stubborn, too vain, too independent.
I often try to do too much, too fast. I sometimes assume
I know everything, when in fact I know so little. Today,
the day the donations arrived, I saw plenty of evidence of
these facts.

*But perhaps knowing my failings is at least a
beginning. I can only have faith that I will learn and
grow, and that I will become a stronger, better person
here, despite the disappointments and hardships . . . not to
mention the "flying rats"!*

Christy closed her diary. It had been quite a day. She
thought of the grand piano in the main room downstairs and
smiled. She knew Miss Alice was right about the donations.
But now that they had the piano, Christy was awfully glad
they were going to get a chance to use it. A party—a "jollification," as Ruby Mae called it—would be just the thing to dis-
tract the children from the recent pranks and to show them
that they had nothing to fear from the mission. Perhaps she'd
invite the children over to the mission house after school on
Friday to help decorate for the party.

Maybe after that, Christy thought hopefully, the strange
pranks would end at last, for once and for all.

$\mathcal{S}even$

SHE IS SO BEAUTIFUL, WRAIGHT THOUGHT. LIZETTE HOL-combe had to be the prettiest girl in the whole, wide state of Tennessee.

He stood in the corner of the mission house parlor with Lundy and Zach and Smith. Miz Christy had invited all the students in after school finished today, so they could help her decorate for the big jollification tomorrow night.

He didn't see as there was any point in going to the party. He couldn't dance worth a hoot. And with his dulcimer all broken to bits, he couldn't play along with Jeb and the preacher and the other music makers. Besides, Lizette would be so beautiful that everyone would want to dance with her. John Spencer, for one. Wraight knew John was sweet on her.

Wraight wondered if John knew pretty things to say to Lizette, the things girls liked. Fancy words about flowers and birds and love. Wraight didn't know any of that sugar-sweet romancing talk. About the only thing he knew to get Lizette's attention was to throw snowballs at her. That always made her laugh, all right.

He'd gone and made a fool of himself when she was trying to help him with his spelling. He'd growled at her like an old bear because he couldn't understand what she was trying to explain.

When that happened—and it happened a whole lot at school—he felt all tight and coiled up inside. He got angry and did things he didn't mean to do, just like his Pa did things he didn't mean to do sometimes.

Wraight watched while Lizette and Bessie and Ruby Mae tried on hats out of the barrel of clothes the mission had for sale. Lizette put on a big floppy straw one with a pink flower on it.

"What do you think, Wraight?" she called to him. "Do I look like a city gal?"

"You look . . ." Wraight hesitated. He glanced over to Lundy for help, but Lundy just gave his usual smirk. "You look fine."

Lizette sort of half smiled, and Wraight breathed a sigh of relief. She was talking to him, at least, so that must mean she wasn't still mad about the way he'd practically bitten her head off when she'd tried to help him with his spelling. That was something, anyway.

Lundy elbowed him. "Why is it you get all tongue tied 'round Lizette? You sweet on her or somethin'?"

"I ain't sweet on nobody."

"John Spencer's got his eye on her, anyways," Lundy said. "'Course, why she'd pay any mind to that puny little varmint—"

"Don't talk that way about John," Zach spoke up. "He ain't so bad."

Lundy socked Zach in the shoulder, hard. "Hush up, weasel face. I ain't talkin' to you."

"Don't hit Zach," Wraight said, clenching his fist. "Never."

Lundy stepped closer, until he was just inches from Wraight's face. "You a-tellin' me what to do?"

Wraight stared past Lundy. He clenched his teeth. The anger boiled up inside him. But he didn't say a word.

"Thought so."

Wraight leaned back against the wall. Lundy was three inches taller than he was and much heavier. He never lost a fight, never, and Wraight knew there was no point in starting one now. Lundy was mean. And he was a good shot. Too good, though not as good as Wraight. Still, around the school, what Lundy wanted, Lundy got. Everybody did what he said, even Wraight. That's just the way it was.

Across the room, Lizette and Ruby Mae were dancing with each other, giggling and carrying on the way girls did. Miz Christy was helping some of the littlest children hang up drawings they'd made for decorations. Miss Ida, the grouchy one with the sharp tongue, was rushing about with a feather duster.

"Want to dance, Wraight?" Lizette called as she whirled past, nearly knocking over a hat rack. She had a scarf around her neck. It flowed behind her, just like a flag in the wind. It was the color of her eyes, as dark and big as night itself.

He wanted to say something just right, when she whirled past again, but all he could think of was, "I can't dance."

He wished so badly that he still had his dulcimer. He'd played it for her once, under a tree during recess. He'd sung a ballad his ma had taught him, one with all the fancy words about love and such that he didn't know how to say himself.

When he was singing or playing his music, everything made sense. He felt smart, like his feelings got shaped into notes. He couldn't spell, couldn't add, but he could make the four strings of his dulcimer sing as sweet as the first spring bluebird. And he wasn't exactly sure, but it had seemed to him that when he played, Lizette had looked at him in a different way. His heart got all stirred up just remembering it.

Of course, he didn't have his dulcimer, not anymore. His pa had smashed it good one night when the moonshine had gotten the better of him. Wraight could still remember that night like it had just happened. It made him knot up inside, just thinking about it. His pa had been mad at him because he hadn't chopped enough wood to keep the fire going.

"You ain't got a lick of sense in you, boy," Pa'd screamed, and then he'd grabbed the dulcimer right out of Wraight's hands. He'd held it high up in the air, waving it back and forth. "I'll get me some firewood right quick," he'd said, his voice all slow and dark with the moonshine.

Then, while Wraight had watched in horror, he'd slammed the little dulcimer against the table. It had broken into a hundred pieces. Splinters of wood covered the floor. It was like watching a living thing die, right before your eyes.

Wraight had tossed the pieces of wood into the fireplace for kindling. He hadn't cried. Hadn't said a word. There wasn't any point in crying.

He'd kept the strings, though. Why, he didn't know. He just couldn't let them go.

He gazed over at the new piano. Miz Christy had been mighty proud about getting it for the mission. She'd said the piano was full of wires inside, long ones. When you pushed on one of the little white or black boxes in a long row—she'd called them keys—a sound happened.

It would pleasure him something fierce to be able to play that big instrument. If he could get a sound out of it, even learn a song or two, maybe then Lizette would listen. Maybe she'd remember how he'd sung and played for her before.

He made his way over to the piano bench. "What are you up to, Wraight Holt?" Lundy called.

Wraight cringed. Lundy was like a dark shadow he could never get rid of. Always causing trouble, always looking to make life harder than it already was. Lundy hated the other students, hated the school, hated Miz Christy. Come to think of it, there wasn't much Lundy Taylor did seem to like. How many times had Wraight heard Lundy talk about getting rid of the school, and Miz Christy with it?

But the truth was sometimes Wraight felt that way too.

"I'm just lookin', is all," Wraight called back to Lundy. "Let me be."

He eased onto the bench. It was slippery. He let his fingers slide over the white keys. They were smooth too. Miz Christy had said they were made of ivory, from elephants' tusks, but he hardly saw how that was possible. She'd said tusks were sharp, like knives. And these keys were as smooth and cool as ice.

Gently he pressed down on a key. Nothing happened. No sound. Nothing like the sweet, sad twang of a dulcimer string.

He pressed again. This time a sound did come—a low, smooth, easy sound that made him start. It came from deep in the belly of the piano, far from his touch. How could that be?

He moved his hand far up the keys. Again he pushed. This time the sound was sweet and high like a raindrop hitting a pool of water. He blinked. It was a plain and simple miracle, near as he could figure.

"Miss Ida," Lundy's taunting voice met his ears. "Wraight Holt is playing on that there music maker."

Miss Ida bustled over and slapped at Wraight's hand. "Get away from there," she said. "That's for people who know how to play. People who've had lessons, which I venture to say you have not."

She slammed the black lid and the magic keys disappeared from view as if they'd never been there. Behind him, Wraight heard Lundy's snarling laugh. Wraight glanced across the room. Lizette was standing with John. She was watching Wraight, and the look in her eyes was nothing like the look he remembered from that day under the tree.

He knew all too well what that look was. Her eyes said she felt sorry for him.

⌐#⌐

"Isn't this the perfect evening for a party?" Christy said to David as they walked along the porch of the mission house.

It was late Saturday afternoon, and the open house was already underway. The sun had just begun to sink. Its brilliant red rays seemed to set the mission house windows on fire. The day had been surprisingly warm for March. Patches of snow still remained, but much of it had melted, turning the yard to mud. Nevertheless, families were already gathering in the yard, laughing and hugging and gossiping.

"Jeb Spencer's already got his dulcimer going," David said. "I'm going to have to round up my ukulele so we can get a duet started."

"The yard's not exactly the best place for dancing," Christy pointed out. "I'd planned on the party taking place inside." She grinned. "Of course, I'm sure Miss Ida would be very relieved if everybody stayed out here."

"The temperature will drop soon enough," David said. "Then everyone will head inside." He paused to gaze at her, just long enough that Christy felt a blush creep up her neck. "By the way," David said, "have I mentioned how very nice you look tonight?"

Christy adjusted the blue bow in her hair. "You look pretty nice yourself," she said shyly just as Ruby Mae came out the front door.

David cleared his throat. "Well, I guess I should go find my ukulele," he said. He nudged Christy with his elbow. "Think later on we could talk you into playing a tune or two on the piano?"

"I'm not so sure that's a good idea, Preacher," Ruby Mae said. "Miz Christy was a-practicin' this afternoon. Scraped my eardrums somethin' fierce."

Christy laughed. "I am a little rusty."

"After all the work it took getting that piano inside the mission house, I can't bear to think it's going to go to waste," David said. "We'd better find somebody around here who can play it."

While David went to find his ukulele, Ruby Mae and Christy watched the party from the porch. Soon Fairlight joined them. She was wearing a lavender crocus in her hair. Little Guy dozed peacefully in her arms, his head on her shoulder.

"Listen to this," she said to Christy. "*F-a-i-r-l-i-g-h-t.*"

"Fairlight, that's wonderful!" Christy exclaimed. "You really are a quick student."

"I can already spell all the names in the family. 'Cept I keep forgettin' to put that there *h* in 'John.'"

"Where is John, anyway?" Christy asked. "I haven't seen him."

"Over yonder," Ruby Mae said. She pointed toward the schoolhouse. "Moonin' over Lizette, like always."

"Poor John," Fairlight said. "I fear he's pinin' for her bad."

"Crazy thing is," Ruby Mae said, lowering her voice, "Bessie Coburn's had her eye on John ever since school started. Told me every time he says howdy to her she plumb near walks on air the rest of the day."

"Are you sure?" Fairlight asked.

"'Course I'm sure. Bessie's my best friend, and she told me after I promised never to breathe a word of it to nobody—" Ruby Mae's eyes went wide. "Confound it all! I'd best be movin' on, before my mouth gets me into any more trouble."

Without another word, she dashed off. Fairlight and Christy laughed as they watched her go.

"Looks like David found his ukulele," Christy said, pointing across the yard.

David and Jeb were sitting next to each other on two overturned crates. As they strummed and sang, more and more people began to clap and dance, wheeling in circles on the muddy grass.

"Jeb loves that dizzifyin' music," Fairlight said. "He'll strum all night long if'n we let him."

"I have the feeling David will too," Christy said.

Miss Alice poked her head out the door. "This seems to have turned into an outdoor party," she said.

"Oh, they'll be in soon enough, Miz Alice," Fairlight said. "Once the dark falls and the air starts a-chillin.'"

A tiny, bent woman passed by the porch. She was leaning on a wooden walking stick for support. She paused, tapping her stick on the porch railing to get Christy's attention.

"Granny O'Teale," Christy exclaimed. Not too long ago, Granny would never have dared set foot at the mission. Christy was very pleased to see her here tonight.

"For a city gal," Granny said, "you give a mighty fine jollification."

"Thank you, Granny," Christy said. "I'm awfully glad you came."

"There's food and such a-comin', right?"

"Oh, yes. Lots of it."

"Then I reckon I'm glad I came too."

Christy watched Granny hobble off. "Wasn't this a wonderful idea, Miss Alice?" Christy asked.

"Yes, it was," Miss Alice agreed. "A fine idea. By the way, I'll be back in the kitchen with Miss Ida if you need me."

Watching the children and adults clapping and dancing, their voices raised in song, Christy felt a warm glow. Cutter Gap might have seen its share of feuds and fighting over the years, but on a night like tonight, with the stars glistening and the music soaring, it seemed as if nothing could go wrong.

"Who's that over yonder?" Fairlight asked. She pointed to the bottom of the ridge, where four figures had emerged from the trees. They were barely visible in the waning light.

"Looks like Wraight and Zach," Christy said.

"Lundy and Smith too," Fairlight said. "Hope they're not here to make trouble."

The four boys marched slowly across the yard.

Lizette caught sight of Wraight and waved. "Wraight!" she called out. "I didn't think you'd come!"

Near the edge of the circle of dancers, Wraight paused to see where the voice was coming from. "Lizette?" he called, peering into the darkening twilight.

"Over here!" Lizette called from the schoolhouse.

Wraight spun around in the direction of her voice. As he turned, he bumped shoulders with one of the dancers and lost his balance. He landed on his hands and knees in a patch of thick mud. Instantly, the music and dancing stopped. Everyone turned to stare at Wraight. After a moment, the whole group broke into gales of laughter.

"That a new dance step, Wraight?" called Bob Allen.

Wraight tried to wipe his hair out of eyes, but he only succeeded in drawing a stripe of mud across his cheek and starting a whole new round of laughter.

"He never were much for dancin'," said Ruby Mae, giggling so hard she had to wipe tears from her eyes.

Christy could see how embarrassed poor Wraight was. As he struggled to his feet, his legs and hands caked with mud, she ran over to help him.

"Don't pay any attention to them, Wraight," she said, taking his arm. "Let's go on inside. I'll get you a towel and you can clean up."

"Don't need none of your help!" Wraight cried, yanking free of her grasp. His eyes burned. "Get away from me!"

"Really," Christy said gently, "I'll get you a towel and you'll be good as new, I promise. Don't be embarrassed. By the end of the evening, I'll bet you almost everybody will have some mud on them."

"I ain't embarrassed," Wraight shot back. He glared at her with such fury that Christy backed away. Without another word, he stomped off toward the mission house.

After a few moments of silence, Jeb and David started playing again. Before long, the dancing was in full swing and Wraight's fall was forgotten.

But no matter how hard she tried, Christy could not forget the look of anger in his eyes.

Eight

WRAIGHT RAN INTO THE MISSION HOUSE BECAUSE IT WAS the only place he could think of where he could hide from the laughter and the stares. He'd looked like a complete fool out there, in front of all of Cutter Gap. Worst of all, he'd looked like a fool in front of Lizette.

He felt the rage inside him like a wild animal clawing to come out. He wanted to hurt something, or maybe even somebody.

He knew it was wrong to feel like this. But he couldn't seem to help it.

There were noises coming from the kitchen. He heard women's voices. The parlor was empty. He leaned against the wall, trying to catch his breath. He was covered with mud. It was on the floor, on the wall, anywhere he touched. What a sight he must have made out there in the yard. Was it any wonder they'd all laughed?

It didn't used to be this way. For as long as Wraight could remember, he'd been the one the other children had looked up to—not the one they laughed at. They'd patted him on the back, shook his hand, tried to be his friend. He could hunt better and shoot better and play the dulcimer better than any of them, and they all knew it.

But ever since the mission school had come around, things had changed. Not a day went by that Miz Christy, with her numbers and her letters and her books, didn't manage to make him feel like a fool. When he felt like that, the anger boiled in him like a kettle on a fire, so hot it burned inside.

He'd known he shouldn't have come to the open house tonight. He'd told Lundy a thousand times he didn't want to. But Lundy had told Wraight he was coming, like it or not. Lundy was hoping to get hold of some moonshine and have a time of it.

Besides, Zach had wanted to come so bad. Their ma and pa weren't coming, and the only way Zach could come was if Wraight did too. He'd practically begged Wraight. How could he have said no? He would do anything for Zach, and Zach would do anything for him. So that was that. Wraight had agreed to come.

He glanced down at his legs. His feet and hands were covered with mud. He wiped his hands on his shirt, but that just made things worse. He had to get out of here. He'd grab Zach and make him head on home. He wondered—if he went back outside, would the laughter start all over again?

Wraight's eyes fell on the big, gleaming piano. The top was propped open with some kind of stick. He started for the door, but something held him back, like a hand grabbing hold of his thoughts.

If he went over to that piano, he'd see the insides. See what made it work.

Slowly Wraight approached the piano, as if it were alive.

His feet left big footprints of mud. He glanced toward the kitchen. He was safe. No one was coming. Miss Ida, who'd shooed him away yesterday, was nowhere around.

He looked inside the piano and gasped. He saw wires, more than anyone could count, tight and long. He touched one with a muddy finger. So many more strings than his dulcimer!

Wraight stepped over to the bench. Even that was a sight to behold, all shiny and smooth. He sat down, almost without knowing what he was doing.

The little key things were lined up like soldiers. Black were thinner than white. He rested a finger on one, then slowly let it sink down. A soft whisper of a sound, like a dove's coo, came out of the piano's insides.

Another key, this one black. He touched it softly, too, not wanting to draw attention. This time the sound was a low grumble, like thunder at the end of a storm.

Something inside him changed. The boiling kettle of anger cooled. His guts weren't all twisted and tight anymore. He could feel the hate dripping away, the way it always did when he played his music.

How many times had he gone to his dulcimer when he'd felt angry? He remembered all those times he and his pa had nearly come to blows. The only thing that would make everything go away was playing and playing till he forgot what it was that had him so riled. He missed that. He hadn't known how much till just now.

Wraight ran his fingers gently up and down the whole keyboard. It was sweet, how the keys gave way and then popped back up, ready for more. With his eyes closed, he did it again, so softly that only a few notes sounded. When he opened his eyes, he looked down in horror to see that he'd left a long trail of mud on the beautiful white keys.

Just then, the front door opened and Miz Christy came in. The preacher was with her, and John Spencer's mama, and a whole lot of others too.

"And here's our new pride and joy," Miz Christy said gaily. "The mission's very own grand piano!"

Then Wraight saw her. Lizette. She was standing at the edge of the group, staring at his muddy clothes with wide, shocked eyes.

Wraight gulped. He had to get out of here, and he had to get out fast. He pushed back the bench and leapt up.

"Wraight!" Miz Christy exclaimed. "There you are." Her eyes dropped to the floor. "Oh, no! Miss Ida's going to have a fit when she sees these footprints!" She rolled her eyes when she noticed the mud on the piano keys. "Wraight," she moaned. "Couldn't you at least have cleaned yourself up first?"

"I—I just wanted to . . ." Wraight muttered.

"I 'spect he thought he could play us all a tune," somebody said, and the laughter started all over again.

"I could play, if'n I had the chance!" Wraight cried. The blood was rushing to his head. He clenched his hands. His stomach churned.

"Well, before you play us a tune, wash up those hands," Miz Christy said. She was smiling, but Wraight knew it wasn't a friendly smile. It was the kind of smile you made when you were laughing on the inside.

He stepped back. The bench fell, crashing to the floor. Wraight pushed his way through the crowd and out the door.

He could feel Lizette's eyes on him. He wanted to hurt something again. And he wanted to run.

For now, he would run. Later—tonight, maybe—there
would be plenty of time for the hurting.

⚬⚬⚬

Christy lay in bed, tossing and turning. It was two in the
morning, but she couldn't seem to get to sleep.

Maybe it was the excitement of the open house. It had
lasted into the wee hours, and everyone had agreed it was
a huge success. To her relief, no windows had been broken,
nothing had caught on fire, no fights had started. And there'd
been no pranks, thank goodness—just lots of joking and
laughing and dancing.

Christy had even danced a couple dances with Dr. Mac-
Neill. Surprisingly, he was a good dancer. And she had to
admit he'd looked very dashing this evening in his fancy coat
and tie. His hair was even neatly combed—for once.

After they were done dancing, Fairlight had whispered
that she'd seen David watching Christy and the doctor very
carefully. "If I didn't know better, Miz Christy," she'd said, "I'd
swear to you that grumpy look on the preacher's face was
pure green envy!"

Christy wondered if Fairlight could be right. Probably
not. Christy and David were just friends—weren't they? And
as for the doctor . . . He couldn't possibly be interested in
Christy romantically. At least, she didn't think so.

Well, she could worry about that another day. The important thing was that the party had been a success. Everyone
had danced and sang and told tall tales and just generally
seemed to enjoy the company of their neighbors. She had

even played a few tunes—badly—on the piano, along with Jeb and David and some of the others.

The thought of the piano made her sigh out loud. Why hadn't she handled things better with Wraight this evening? She hadn't meant to embarrass him about getting the piano dirty, but clearly she had.

Lizette, who was spending the night here at the mission house with Ruby Mae and Bessie, had told Christy not to worry. She'd said that lately, Wraight seemed to have a temper that could flare up like a bonfire. "It isn't your fault, Miz Christy," she'd said sadly. "Near as I can figure, it's nobody's fault."

Well, maybe so. But Christy was the teacher, and she should have known better than to humiliate Wraight when he'd already been embarrassed in front of everyone once that night. Monday, she'd be sure to apologize to him. Not that her apology would probably change anything. But she had to try.

She rolled over onto her side and tried to count sheep. She was on number eighteen when she heard a loud thump. She sat up in bed, waiting to see if she heard anything else.

No, nothing. It was probably Ruby Mae and her two friends, creeping around and making mischief.

Christy closed her eyes and started counting again. This time she made it to sheep number twenty-one before she heard another thud.

She threw back her covers. Those girls were going to keep her up all night unless she put a stop to this. Ruby Mae had promised she and the others would be on their best behavior. Christy smiled as she donned her robe. Come to think of it, this probably was their best behavior.

Christy opened her door. She didn't have a lamp with her,

but the moonlight through the hall window was bright. She heard a creak coming from downstairs, the sound of a footstep on wood. The girls were probably in the kitchen, searching for the last of Miss Ida's oatmeal cookies.

Christy eased open the door to Ruby Mae's bedroom. To her shock, all three girls were sleeping peacefully. Ruby Mae was snoring away.

Her hand trembling slightly, Christy closed the door. Across the hall, Miss Ida's door was closed, which probably meant she was sound asleep too. She'd said she was exhausted after all the frantic preparations for the open house.

From somewhere downstairs came another thump. Christy's heart raced. If it wasn't Miss Ida, and it wasn't the girls, who could be downstairs at this hour?

Slowly, as quietly as she could, Christy crept down the stairs. Each step brought her a little closer to her fear.

She heard a creak. "Miss Ida?" she called in a hoarse whisper.

No one answered. Christy tried to swallow, but her throat was tight and dry.

At last she reached the bottom of the stairs. Moonlight filled the parlor with a milky glow. Nothing moved. No one seemed to be there.

She took two steps across the cold, wooden floor. She held her breath, and then she heard it—someone else's breathing.

Christy spun around.

Near the piano, she saw him. He was tall and menacing, his face hidden in shadow. She could just make out the glimmer of a silver knife, poised high in the air over the open piano. The knife came down, in slow motion, and disappeared deep inside the piano. There was a sharp, metallic noise as it sliced through a wire.

"No!" Without thinking, Christy dashed toward the figure. Suddenly she realized who it was. She came to an abrupt stop inches away from the intruder.

"Wraight?" she whispered.

His eyes shone in the moonlight with a terrible anger, like nothing she'd ever seen before. He lifted the knife again, high over Christy's head.

"No, Wraight!" she cried, and as the knife came down, she grabbed for his arm with all her might.

Nine

CHRISTY LOCKED HER HANDS ONTO WRAIGHT'S STRONG
arm. The knife gleamed in the eerie light.

"It's been you all along, Wraight, hasn't it?" she whispered.

She felt his arm go limp. His eyes filled with tears.

"Don't do it, Wraight!" a boy's voice cried.

Christy spun around to see Zach, climbing through a
half-open window on the other side of the room. He dashed
across the space and threw himself against his big brother,
sobbing frantically.

Wraight let the knife drop to the floor. "I told you not to
follow me again," he said softly.

Zach clung to Wraight, his arms tight around the older
boy's waist. "He wouldn't never hurt you, Miz Christy," Zach
said. Tears streamed down his face. "He was just mad, is all.
Like the other times."

Christy stared into Wraight's face, hoping to find an
explanation there. But all she saw was a confused, unhappy
boy.

"Was it you all those times, Wraight?" she asked. "The ink and the message on the school?"

He hung his head but didn't answer.

"And that time I was walking home from the Spencers'— was that you too?"

Wraight nodded slightly.

"But I was sure it was Zach," Christy said. "I thought Lundy was putting him up to it—"

Wraight looked up. He had a grim half smile on his face. "Do sound like Lundy, don't it?"

Christy touched Zach's shoulder gently. "But Zach, why were you always there? I saw you at the schoolhouse, the night that message was left. And out in the woods . . ."

Wraight held his brother close. "It weren't him. It were me, every time. Zach, he's like my twin or something. Or my— what is it the preacher calls it?—my conch . . . uh, my . . ."

"Conscience," Christy said.

"He knew I was up to no good, and when I wouldn't listen to nothing he had to say, he started following me around." He touched Zach's red cap. "Followed me tonight, too, even though I told him if'n he did I'd make him do my chores for a month."

"Christy?" Miss Ida called from the top of the stairwell. "Do I hear voices down there?"

"Wait here," Christy told the boys. She went to the stairs. Ruby Mae, Bessie, and Lizette were sitting on the top steps, yawning and rubbing their eyes.

"Everything's under control, Miss Ida. Go back to sleep," Christy said. "That goes for you girls too."

"Can't sleep," Ruby Mae said firmly. "You've got us all a-wondering what's goin' on."

"I can sleep just fine, thank you," said Miss Ida. She turned on her heel and went back to her room.

"You girls wait there," Christy instructed.

She went back to Zach and Wraight. "Zach," she said, kneeling down, "I need to talk to your brother for a few minutes, all right? You go on up to the top of the stairs and wait. Some of your school friends are up there."

"Is they . . . girls?"

"I'm afraid so."

Zach moaned. "See what you got me into?" he said to Wraight. He turned to Christy. "He ain't in big trouble, is he, Teacher?"

"Well, he's in trouble," Christy said. "But I wouldn't worry, if I were you."

"If you whop him with a birch switch, he won't cry a lick," Zach said proudly.

"I don't think that will be necessary, Zach," Christy said with a smile. "Now, you go on up."

Zach headed upstairs, and Christy motioned for Wraight to join her on the piano bench. He gazed at her doubtfully.

"Come on, Wraight," Christy said. "We need to talk."

After a moment, he sat down awkwardly beside her.

Christy took a deep breath, trying to clear her thoughts. Moonlight flowed over the piano like liquid silver. Wraight's sharp knife still lay on the floor. She could hear the soft whispers of Zach and the girls on the stairs.

She thought of the spilled ink and the erased chalkboard. She thought of the angry message on the schoolhouse. She thought of her fear—that night in the woods—and again tonight.

She was angry at Wraight. She wanted to tell him that.

Part of her even wanted to scare him, the way he'd scared her. But when she looked at the quiet boy sitting beside her, staring at the piano keys as if they were bars of gold, she wondered if getting angry was the answer. She wanted to help Wraight more than she wanted to get angry at him.

Miss Alice had said that Christy had to understand the mountain people before she would ever be able to help them.

Why would Wraight have turned on Christy? Why, when he seemed so entranced by the piano, would he try to hurt it?

"You know, Wraight," Christy said, "I'll let you in on a little secret. Ever since I came here to the mission, I keep making mistakes. Sometimes I feel like a real fool."

Wraight stared at her, mystified, as if she were speaking in a foreign language. "You?" he said at last. "Make mistakes? Ain't likely."

"It's true," Christy insisted. "Like those donations I got for the mission. I thought they were a good idea, but it turned out Miss Alice was pretty unhappy with me. The way I asked for them wasn't right. And we ended up with things we're going to have a hard time using, like telephone wire." She ran her fingers over the keys. "And, of course, this piano."

"This piano ain't no mistake," Wraight said firmly. "It's the most amazin' thing Cutter Gap ever seen. It's like . . ."

He threw open his arms, searching for the right word. "Like the biggest dulcimer in the whole, wide world, right here, just a-waitin' for someone to help it sing."

Christy played a soft chord, three notes together that lingered in the air. "Then why did you cut that wire, Wraight? Why did you want to hurt the piano?"

For a long time Wraight sat silently, staring at the keyboard. "Sometimes," he said at last, "when you can't have something . . . it just makes you so mad, you feel like you're going to bust up inside."

"But if you'd wanted lessons on the piano, I would have been glad to teach you, Wraight. Not that I'm much of a piano player, mind you. But all you had to do was ask."

Wraight gave a hard laugh. "And make more of a fool of myself than I have already? Not hardly."

"What are you talking about?"

"Like it ain't as plain as the nose on my face."

Christy touched him on the shoulder. "I don't understand, Wraight. Really, I don't. Try to explain it to me."

Wraight thought for a while. "I can't step inside that there schoolhouse," he said, avoiding her gaze, "without sayin' or doin' somethin' so all-fired stupid that I sound like the biggest fool this side of Coldsprings Mountain. The way you're always goin' on about numbers and letters and such, it's enough to make me—"

"What? Make you angry?" Christy asked. At last she was beginning to understand.

"Well, if'n you want the whole truth—" Wraight's voice was harsh. "—some days it makes me want to burn that whole school right to the ground."

Christy nodded. "Sometimes fear makes a person do things he doesn't want to do," she said. "Things he knows are wrong."

Wraight pushed down a key with his index finger and listened. "I reckon," he finally said.

"Lizette tells me you're quite a dulcimer player," Christy said.

"Don't have no dulcimer no more."

"I never could play the piano very well," Christy said. "I

took lessons growing up, but no matter how hard I tried, my fingers just couldn't keep up with the notes." She laughed softly. "One year, when I was eight, we had a recital. All the parents came to hear us. It seemed to me like all of Asheville, North Carolina, was there. Well, my teacher wanted me to play something simple. You know, like 'Twinkle, Twinkle, Little Star.' You've heard that, haven't you?"

Christy plunked out the first few notes of the song, and Wraight nodded.

"But of course, I had other things on my mind. I wanted to impress everyone with my incredible talent. So I decided to play one of my favorite hymns: 'What a Friend We Have in Jesus.'"

This time she played the first notes of the hymn. Wraight watched her fingers, fascinated.

"Well, needless to say, I got up there to play, and I froze. I played about three notes, looked out at all those faces in the audience, and the fear just took over."

"What happened then?" Wraight asked.

"I'm very embarrassed to report that I threw up all over my piano teacher's favorite rug."

Wraight burst out laughing. "Miz Christy, that is the saddest tale I ever did hear! You wouldn't tell me a whopper, now, would you?"

"Cross my heart. It's the truth. And the really sad thing is that I stopped taking lessons after that. I was so afraid of failing that I just gave up. I've always regretted it." She sighed. "Now it seems like I can hardly get a note out of this piano."

"Try," Wraight said softly. His voice was almost pleading.

Christy cleared her throat. "Well, here goes nothing."

Slowly and painfully, she began to play "What a Friend

We Have in Jesus." All too often, she hit a wrong note that made her wince, but she kept going because Wraight seemed to want her to. He was watching her fingers as if he were in a trance.

Halfway through, she struggled again and again with the same chord, but she simply couldn't find the right note.

"Maybe that's enough. I don't want to ruin your hearing," she said. "I'm sorry. I just can't seem to get it right."

"Could I . . . could I give it a whirl?" Wraight whispered.

Christy slid off the bench. "Be my guest."

Wraight stared at the keys, deep in concentration. He arranged his fingers carefully, then pressed them all down at once.

The first chord of the old gospel hymn rang out. Wraight closed his eyes as if he'd witnessed a miracle. Then, slowly and with great care, he began to play the same piece Christy had struggled through. He only missed a few notes. Christy watched in amazement. She felt the way she had when she was teaching Fairlight Spencer to read—as if all she'd had to do was open a door and send Wraight on his way.

She thought of all the times she'd been frustrated with Wraight, and with the other slow learners in her class. How wrong she'd been about him. Perhaps different students learned in different ways. It was her job to find the door that would allow each one into the place where Wraight had just ventured.

When he was done, she applauded. "That was amazing, Wraight. Absolutely amazing."

"Ain't nothin'. You just sound 'em out, one at a time. Low notes are down at that end. High ones up yonder." He shrugged. "It's easy enough."

"Tell that to my old piano teacher." Christy laughed. "You have a real gift, Wraight. I was wondering—if I could locate some piano instruction books, how would you like to come over to the mission house after school and practice? I could teach you what I know, which isn't much. But then you'd be pretty much on your own."

To her shock, Wraight shook his head firmly. "Can't," was all he said.

"But I thought you'd . . ."

Once again, Miss Alice's words about the donations came back to her: *"There's a strong mountain code, you see. No one wants to owe anyone for anything. These people don't respect anyone who can't earn his own way."*

"Wraight," Christy said, "suppose you did odd jobs around the mission to pay for your lessons? It would be a way to pay us back for the damage to the piano too. We'll need to replace that wire. I know David's got a lot of work around here left to do. He wants to build a better barn for Goldie and Prince and Old Theo, to start with. And one of these days, he may have a telephone he needs help hooking up."

Wraight scratched his chin. "So it'd be fair and square-like? I'd be working for the time I spent on the piano?"

"Fair and square."

"I s'pose I could manage that," he said casually, but Christy could see the excitement in his eyes.

"Good. It's a deal, then. And Wraight?"

"Yes'm?"

"If you feel angry like that again, will you come to me and talk about it?"

"No'm."

Christy sighed. "But why not?"

"Don't need to talk with you, if'n I got this here piano to talk to." He looked up at her hopefully. "You reckon I could play real quiet-like for another minute or two? I was hopin' maybe I could practice up to play for Lizette."

"I have an even better idea," Christy said. "Wait here."

She went upstairs. Zach was asleep on the landing. Ruby Mae and Bessie had gone back to bed. But Lizette was sitting on the top step, wide awake.

"Have you been listening?" Christy asked.

"Oh, no, Miz Christy. I ain't no eaves-dropper."

"Of course, you might have accidently overheard a thing or two."

Lizette gave a sheepish grin. "Well, maybe just a wee bit."

"If you're in the mood for a concert," Christy said, "I happen to know a fine piano player who's in the mood to give one."

Lizette ran down the stairs. A moment later, Christy heard the slow, careful strains of "What a Friend We Have in Jesus" coming from the parlor. There were a few missed notes and some awkward pauses, but she'd never heard the old hymn played with more love.

About Catherine Marshall

Catherine Marshall LeSourd (1914–1983), a *New York Times* bestselling author, is best known for her novel *Christy*. Based on the life of her mother, a teacher of mountain children in poverty-stricken Tennessee, *Christy* captured the hearts of millions and became a popular CBS television series. As her mother reminisced around the kitchen table at Evergreen Farm, Catherine probed for details and insights into the rugged lives of these Appalachian highlanders.

The Christy® of Cutter Gap series, based on the characters of the beloved novel, contains expanded adventures filled with romance, excitement, and intrigue.

Catherine also wrote *Julie*, a sweeping novel of love and adventure, courage and commitment, tragedy and triumph, in a Pennsylvania steel town during the Great Depression.

Catherine's first husband, Peter Marshall, was Chaplain of the U.S. Senate, and her intimate biography of him, *A Man Called Peter*, became an international bestseller and Academy Award Nominated movie. The story shares the power of this dynamic man's love for his God and for the woman he married.

A beloved inspirational writer and speaker, Catherine's enduring career spanned four decades and six continents, and reached over 30 million readers.

CHRISTY'S ADVENTURES CONTINUE IN...

During a furious storm, Christy's student Ruby Mae Morrison and the mission's black stallion disappear into the night. Christy desperately searches for Ruby Mae in the cold, blinding rain. She runs headlong into three angry moonshiners who will stop at nothing to protect their illegal activities.

Will Christy survive this most terrifying test of her faith and courage?

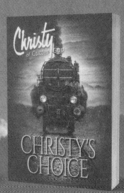